Chanticleer's Wood

Published by Lenka Medlik
©Lenka Medlik 2012

The right of Lenka Medlik to be identified as
the author of this work has been asserted by her
in accordance with the Copyright, Designs and
Patents Act 1988

This book is a work of fiction and the characters
depict no persons living or dead.

ISBN 978-0-9574818-0-0

Chanticleer's Wood

Lenka Medlik

To Geoff

CONTENTS

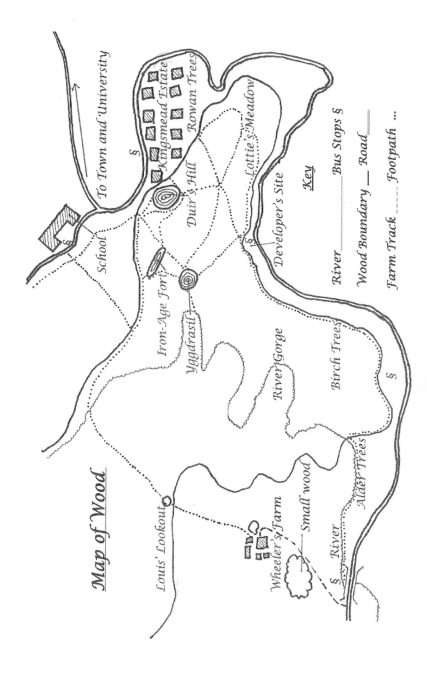

Map of Wood

To Town and University

Kingsmead Estate

Rowan Trees

§

Lottie's Meadow

Duir's Hill

Developer's Site

School

Iron-Age Fort

Yggdrasil

§

River Gorge

Birch Trees

§

Louis' Lookout

Alder Trees

Wheeler's Farm

Small wood

§ River

Key

River ———
Bus Stops §
Wood Boundary —
Road ———
Farm Track - - - -
Footpath .....

1 My Brand New Life

The first day I'd ever had to go to school and Dad was still asleep. I went in and poked him to make sure he was alive, and he snarled and rolled over in bed like a great hibernating bear.

'He had to increase his tablets last night, I think it's really knocked him out,' Mum said as she tried to find something to wear. 'Are you sure you'll be okay on your own this morning?'

'I'll be fine.' Yeah, well I'd just have to be wouldn't I . Never mind that it was a bit of a change going to a huge comprehensive school from being home-schooled until the age of twelve. Mum was always telling people: 'Oh Louis is so sensible and independent for his age.' It kind of suited her to think that right now.

'Can you see if Lottie's wearing something vaguely reasonable for her first day at nursery?' she begged.

I went in to check the latest outfit my little sister had selected. We'd already been through Mum's flowery shirt I'd taken off the night before, Lottie's Snow White costume and her swimsuit with a sarong thing round the waist. Now she was in her vest and knickers and had my maroon blazer on back to front and was marching round the kitchen. She had stuck the Barbies along the front of the cooker, muttering, 'You're on the waiting list! You're not on the waiting list!' Then she started fiddling with the gas knobs. I grabbed her away and sat her back in front of her weetabix, rescuing my blazer just before it got dolloped with it. Not that I would have minded not being able to wear it, but Mum would not be too thrilled.

'That looked completely bonkers, Lots.'

'I'm a teacher, give me back my uniform!' she shouted, banging loudly on the table with her spoon, splattering milk everywhere.

'Stop it!' I yelled at her. 'Mum, hurry up, I've got to go!' but Mum was going frantic pulling stuff out of her wardrobe. Women and their clothes. 'Listen Lottie, if you wear the clothes I give you and eat your food I'll take you to the playground after school.'

'*Or* right,' she said grudgingly and allowed me to poke her arms and legs into some crumpled dungarees between spoonfuls. Mum came in, looking stressed out.

'Louis, you're a star.'

'I'm off to school for a rest,' I said, and got out while I could.

It was quite nice out, crisp, but sunny, and I thought, maybe school will actually be a good break from home. I took Chestnut Avenue part of the way we'd gone the night before, then branched off left before the shops. Yesterday Lottie and I had been down to get fish and chips for tea with Mum's last ten pounds and that had led to another row with her and Dad. 'Oh, so blow it on junk food!' he'd bellowed and stormed off for the rest of the evening.

Mum had said not to take it to heart, though judging from

her face she had had almost enough of him. 'He doesn't really mean these things, he's just depressed. It's hit him harder than the rest of us, I suppose, it was his own Dad's farm and so on ... he's feeling he's let us down though of course it's not his fault. Those pills should start to kick in in a few days the doc said, then maybe he'll perk up a bit. Also if something comes of those job applications we helped him get in ... though it's been a while since. He's probably finding it really hard that I'm the breadwinner for the time being and he doesn't have much of a role, not even looking after Lottie now we've got this last minute cancellation at the uni nursery.'

She'd said she'd order some food online, so I hoped there'd be something to eat when I got home tonight. It certainly was a bit different to our farm we'd just been turfed off. There was always tons of food in the kitchen there, half of it we grew ourselves. We'd eaten it on this big old pine table that wouldn't fit into the new flat; instead we'd had to use a fold-up camping table. Tea had been grim even without Dad.

As for my room, as Mum said, it was more like a cupboard: you could just fit in my crappy secondhand bunk-bed with 'storage/study area' under it and squeeze round the sides. It'd be hard to have any new friends stay over. If, in fact, I met any new friends at this school. Last night I'd kept a look-out for other kids on the estate. We'd passed some people doing skateboarding up a ramp leading to Swallow Court. All the blocks of flats on the Kingsmead Estate were called after something to do with nature: ours was Oaklands, next door was Nightingale Court, like it was some lovely field with trees and birds or something.

One of the skateboarders had called out 'look over there guys, two new girlies!'

'They're stupid, you're not a girl,' Lottie had said indignantly. I'd told her not to look at them and just keep walking. I'd felt a bit of an idiot in fact as I was still wearing an old flowery shirt of Mum's from when I'd been helping her clear up the flat earlier as all my other gear was still in bin-liners.

Walking past the ramp this morning I could see a few people with the same uniform as mine. (I'd never worn uniform in my life before - this one was seriously bad.) One was a fat boy with headphones on, then there were a group of younger girls all with really short skirts and loads of make-up, and a few other guys who in fact looked quite scary. I avoided everyone and kept my head down, my heart sinking steadily.

Even if I'd wanted to have someone back to my room there was the small problem of Chanticleer. He was our rooster from the farm who had stopped crowing round about the time the farm stock was auctioned off and the hens were taken by a farmer who didn't need a rooster. He'd just sat there all pathetic and somehow got forgotten as there was so much to do and he wasn't making his usual racket. The day of the move was really grim, when the lorries came to take away our rare breed animals. It was almost as bad as leaving it ourselves. They were like, really bewildered, as they were herded into the lorry, and protesting, like they knew something big was up. My favourite llama, Coppertop, who was slightly less dopey than the others, just stared at me like I'd betrayed him. I couldn't explain to him he was one of the lucky ones; our farm hadn't actually been infected with foot and mouth, so he could go to a real new home rather than the llama pens in the sky. But we'd gone bankrupt because no visitors could get near us for a very long time, so they'd had to go.

On the day of the move, when I realised Chanticleer was still there I decided not to say anything but smuggled him out in a box marked 'Fragile.' The only place to hide him had been under my bunk hidden by the rest of my junk. He still hadn't got his voice back which was just as well, but had not eaten much at all either. It was like he was pining. I knew the feeling. I had no idea what I was going to do with him.

So I had all that to deal with as well as Dad's illness, them rowing, and now starting school. Pining was a bit of a luxury at this stage I felt like telling Chanticleer.

Right now I was feeling seriously scared. School sounded like the weirdest, most punishing invention I could imagine. Home-schooling meant I'd learnt stuff without any big deal, fitted around our life on the farm; Mum was pretty good at getting me to do half my lessons outdoors and quite often made an outing out of whatever project I was into; quite a few of the other kids from nearby farms did the same so I had plenty of mates. But the idea of being herded into one big building for the whole day with a huge number of strangers, doing one lesson after another in classrooms with teachers sounded unbelievably bad. A bit like battery-farming must feel for animals I guess. Some of the old school stories I'd read could make boarding school seem a bit more cosy; but I knew they were old-fashioned and made-up anyway. Sometimes we'd passed the outsides of schools on our trips to towns and cities and they made me think of prisons.

Still, we hadn't even had time to visit this school yet, as leaving the farm had happened so suddenly. You never knew, it might turn out to be a really cool place. A little way out of the estate, the road ran along the bottom of a field that rose gradually, back to the woods behind our flats. It looked very tempting compared to what lay ahead, but I kept going until I reached Kingsmead College. It was another example of poshed-up naming, I thought. 'College' made it sound old and full of clever people, like Oxford or somewhere; as I discovered, the reality was pretty different.

2 Problem Parents

Outside, the building was square and horrible, like a concrete factory. Inside, it was a war zone, with people pushing and shoving, shouting and screaming; things flew through the air; kids were fighting on the floor. It was hot and airless and I so did not want to be there. I'd never been inside a school before so I didn't know if this was normal. My parents couldn't have realised what they were sending me to either. Some support would have been a help right then - even Dad would have been better than nothing. I had to ask about six people where my classroom was, and ended up being last in. The only desks were right at the front, next to the teacher's. Probably the safest place anyway, I thought as something small and hard hit the back of my head. A rubber bounced to the floor. When I turned round one of the skateboarders said: 'Hiya new girl, where's the big girl's flowery blouse then?'

'Shut up Farrow and sit down,' said the teacher, Mr. Simon. He took the register, all in surnames. 'You're new aren't you?' I nodded. 'Well, welcome to the school - and good luck.' Did he think I'd need it? We got new exercise books; straightaway there were a dozen paper planes whizzing through the air. Mr Simon was the History teacher and this was the first lesson, which was okay by me as it used to be my favourite subject after Biology. But it turned out we were going to do the Tudors which I'd just spent ages on last year. So I knew most of it. I made the mistake of answering a question about the Armada, and behind me Farrow started up, 'Clever clogs then are we, new girlie?' So I said nothing after that. Mr Simon had no real control over them, just told them to shut up all the time.

Then it was break and everyone headed straight for some drinks machines. I didn't have any money so went outside into the playground. It was just another big tarmac space, with some bike sheds at one end and a few benches. No one talked to me and I didn't feel able to go and barge into their groups. It was the same at lunchtime. The food was chips, baked beans and something in breadcrumbs. A lot of it ended up on the floor. It was a big relief to leave the canteen. I decided to explore the rest of the building.

Turning down an empty corridor with ripped vinyl I came to the library which wasn't too bad. At least it was quiet, as there was no one in there, and there were masses of books and magazines. I found a comic and got so stuck into it I didn't hear the afternoon bell and was late; no one seemed to care though. I'd been prepared for school to be all organised and punctual; it certainly wasn't like the school stories I'd read.

The afternoon seemed to drag on forever. Finally an ear-splitting bell led to a slamming of lids, scraping of chairs and repetition of the morning's madness. I couldn't wait to get home and be with Mum and Lottie again. I left as quickly as I could and was home in ten minutes.

I ran up the four flights of stairs and knocked on the peeling paintwork of our front door. There was no answer. I realised that I didn't know when they were due home; must be why Mum had given me my own key. Slowly, I let myself in and went through to the sitting room. Dad was asleep on the sofa with the afternoon play on the radio blaring away. He opened his eyes when I shouted hello and looked a bit puzzled, almost like he couldn't remember who I was. 'Hello ... son,' he said and went back to sleep. Great.

In the kitchen there was a white mountain of carrier bags from Tesco that Mum had ordered online. They were just sitting there, with frozen stuff starting to thaw. He hadn't bothered to put them away. I stuck the fridge stuff in the fridge and ate a couple of bananas. Then decided I had had enough of this: it was still sunny outside. So I grabbed some ginger biscuits and got out.

The back door in the basement led out into the yard. I'd been going to check this out but there was a guy pottering about in and out of a flat with a skip outside and I felt like being by myself. I thought it would be a very long time before I got used to the crowds that fill up a school; it had done my head in a bit.

There was the grassy bank that reached up to the wood, so I started climbing. It was hard work at first as it was so steep, but I was in the trees almost straightaway and it was shady and cool. The trees were all sorts: small ones with red berries at the edge of the estate, I didn't know what they were called; then lots of silver birches; further on were oaks and chestnuts. I spotted a few conkers gleaming among the leaves, but made myself wait to get them on the way back. There was no path but it was easy going between the large trees. When I was about as high as the roof of Oaklands the slope leveled out and gave way to dips and hollows and low mounds. I came to a larger clearing with grass in it, and a fallen tree that was in the sun. A good place for a snack. It was hot, so I took off my blazer, then my shoes and socks. The grass was soft and springy beneath my bare feet. A grasshopper landed on me and I kept very still. It was so quiet here. The estate, our flat, school, all seemed like a bad dream. I could have been back in the fields on our old farm. I munched on the ginger biscuits slowly, feeling a little breeze on my damp face. The wind rustled the leaves above my head. Looking up at the big old trees, I immediately wanted to climb them.

At first this was easier said than done. Picking a tall, broad oak at the edge of the clearing, I searched around for a foothold. There was a sort of little hollow I could reach with shoots sprouting out that made it like a sad old face with a beard. I pulled myself up by this and wedged my bare feet into a crack in the bark; then I could reach the lowest branch. From then on it was straightforward and I was climbing up and up into the sunlight like on a ship's mast. It was windier up there and the branches swayed like a boat. I was nearly at the top now; it was great. Out of breath, I sat astride a branch as thick as my body and leant against the trunk. I could see right over the estate from here, and beyond: to the grey town and in the distance, the white new blocks of the University where Mum and Lottie were. My school was hidden from sight around the shoulder of the hill and that was fine by me. I was on top of the world; it was like it was my castle, my escape from school and the Drearyville Estate as I had decided to call it. I could come back here all the time, with things to do.

In the distance a window in the University glinted brightly as the sun sank lower. I wondered if it was the window of Mum's new office and whether she'd be able to see me if she had binoculars. She would probably be back soon and wanting us to tell all about our days. She had said she'd make a tortilla tonight, one of my favourites. I climbed down and hurried hungrily home.

But there was no appetising smell of herbs and potatoes frying when I got in. Instead there was Dad in the kitchen banging about in the cupboards with pan lids clattering on the floor.

'Hi Dad. Where's Mum and Lottie?' I asked. He grunted and got up red-faced from squatting by the cupboards.

'Where've you been? I just had a call from your mother: she says she's got a late meeting today and Lottie can have tea at nursery, so I'm to do an omelette for you and me.'

'Oh ... okay. Spanish Omelette like Mum was going to do?'

'Don't be daft. When have I ever made one of those? It'll be a plain English omelette with cheese and onion if you're lucky, and if we've got some. You and I are probably going to have to get used to fending for ourselves now your mother's got this job.' He bent down again to his clattering. Not a word about how was school.

The omelette stuck to the pan because he forgot to oil it, so it was all in pieces and pretty leathery. But I scoffed it down as I was hungry from being outside, and he had tried to do something for a change. 'Are you feeling better yet?' I tried, once we'd finished and he was taking his teatime tablets.

He looked wary. 'So so.'

'Are your pills kicking in yet?'

'Who knows?' he said shortly as he swigged down the pills with some water. 'Pills aren't going to make any difference. I'm not going to suddenly start singing and dancing when I've lost everything and can't even support my family now, am I, just by popping a few pills. I'm taking them to keep your mother and the doctor happy, basically. That reminds me. He's coming round tonight so you'd better go to your room then.'

'Okay. Dad?'

'What?'

'You could, like, have a shave before he comes. Make you look less like a tramp.'

'Thanks a lot.' Just then there was a knock at the door. It was Dr Williams from the health centre. Mum had said we were lucky to get him as he really cared about people like Dad who wouldn't go to the doctor, and he did home visits which were nearly unheard of these days.

I left them to it and went and looked at the tree poster that was the only thing I'd managed to find wall space for in my room. At least they hadn't given us homework the first day. I saw that the trees at the edge of the waste ground were rowan trees, also called mountain ash. 'Sorbus aucuparia' was the Latin name, and it said 'aucuparia' came from words meaning 'to catch a bird.' They used to use the red berries to bait bird traps with, as birds liked eating them. The trees did well in poor soil and often grew in disturbed areas of land. Like behind these flats in fact. I was interested as Rowan was my middle name, and I'd known it was also the name of a type of tree, but not what it looked like. It was quite an attractive tree to be named after really. My name was an old Scottish one from Dad's side of family. All the men in our family had it as their middle name.

Bird traps reminded me of Chanticleer under the bed. I checked on him. He was just sitting there and looked at me with only one beady eye open. It was getting pretty smelly in there and he hadn't touched the food, so I took it out and changed the water. He needed to get out, anyone would be depressed cooped up in this place. But it would be hard to smuggle him out, and I had no idea where he could go. I put him on the top bunk for a bit so he could see out of the window; but he didn't show any interest, so I returned him to the box after a while and he didn't protest either. Might as well get into bed, I decided, feeling pretty tired suddenly. I was wondering if I was like the rowan tree, able to get by in harsh places. I hoped so, as I felt like I was going to need strength from somewhere.

I was reading in bed when Mum came in. I heard her talking with Dad and the doctor, who left soon after. She ran Lottie a bath, then came into my room.

'Louis, hello, I'm sorry to be so late back. You'll never believe what a day I've had. Endless Inductions, with Fire Safety lectures, Equal Opportunities talks, Meet the Language Department drinks and nibbles and then this late faculty meeting. At least Lottie had a great time at the nursery, they said she'd settled really well. I've got to get her bathed and in bed ready to do it all again tomorrow, so talk to you in the morning, you look as tired as I feel!' She rushed off again. Not a word about my first day.

Later, I was almost asleep when I heard raised voices in the kitchen. 'I am not taking disability allowance!' shouted my father. 'I'm not some pathetic bludger!'

'The doctor said it could be some time -' Mum tried to say.

'Yes it could be the rest of my life. But I'm not milking the system, Sally. I've never taken handouts in my life and I won't start now!' he raged.

'But I can't afford to shop online and buy clothes and pay rent on this dump, all on my mingy lecturer's salary.'

'What's wrong with shopping at the market like you used to? It's much cheaper.'

'I can't drag stuff back from it now without a car, and when am I supposed to get there with a full time job?' she said witheringly. 'You'll just have to help a bit more, whether you feel up to it or not. Look at this place! What've you done here today? Cooked one lousy meal. Not washed up, or put away the shopping or unpacked any more of our boxes from the move. It's just not going to work out unless you make a bit of an effort, however unwell you feel.'

'Oh fine then. Why don't I just top myself and you can

claim the insurance and not have to worry about any of it!'

'Because they don't pay up for suicides stupid!' she exclaimed angrily. I pulled the duvet up round my ears so I didn't have to listen to any more. When she gets into nag mode she can go on and on. But he would drive anyone mad. All my good mood from the woods had gone. I felt like we were in this hell hole for ever and nothing was going to change. I didn't think he was in the slightest bit serious about topping himself. But I'd heard that a few farmers in our situation had done. There was a farm a few miles from ours whose whole dairy herd was destroyed. That sickening burning smell seemed like it had never left my nostrils. Dad hadn't had the destruction of his own animals to deal with, but he'd been told he was clinically depressed - whatever that meant. It was obvious he wasn't right and who knew what he would do.

I tossed and turned for hours, trying to block out the sounds of voices arguing and the visions of burning animals that came back to haunt me. In fact I'd seen more of that on TV than in real life. But I still couldn't get it out of my head at night, and that particular night I had loads of nightmares about fires and people being swallowed up in flames. I felt like death warmed up when I woke in the morning.

3 The Weird Wood

I was heading for being late for school and it was only the second day. Mum and Lottie had already left, thank goodness. Dad was still asleep. There was nothing to stop me having crisps for breakfast, so I did. Then I had a bright idea. I took three Penguin biscuits and an apple and filled a small bottle with water. That way, I thought, I need not come home first after school. I was not exactly going to be missed round here. I could take a direct and less steep route to the woods straight from school, along the edge of the field I'd passed.

Whistling cheerfully, I hurried along Chestnut Avenue, now I had something to look forward to. Just have to try and tune out the hours in between. Reaching the playground I'd promised to take Lottie to, I suddenly felt a bit silly whistling, as there was a girl sitting on the roundabout looking at me like I was a bit of an idiot or something. Or that was how it seemed to me. She was just sitting there, giving it a push every now and then with her foot to make it move. Probably from my school: the uniform looked right, although it was hard to tell as she had no tie or blazer, just a short skirt and aertex games top and plimsolls. Her face was white and thin with quite a pointy nose, and her long dark hair was straggly and loose. She had her large greenish eyes fixed on me, like no one ever told her it was rude to stare. No way was I going to be bothered by that though. I pretended to fiddle with something in my bag as a reason to stop whistling, nothing to do with her of course, and hurried on to school. She didn't move; maybe she was planning on skipping school that day. Not a bad idea. I wondered how you got away with it.

Best not to rock the boat just yet though. So I sat it out for another excruciating day. In some ways it was worse as it was Maths and Chemistry and I was pretty behind in Chemistry and didn't know what the teacher was on about. I only cared about this because Mum said I'd need it later if I wanted to be a Biologist, which I definitely did. In the afternoon it was football, the one subject they took seriously round there, and I was pretty useless at that too, not having had much practice. Again, no one talked to me all day, and I couldn't see anyone I'd want to talk to. I wasn't shy; I would have made an effort if it was worth it, but they all seemed pretty moronic, like Farrow and his mates. There was no sign of the girl from the playground.

All in all I was pretty relieved when the last bell sounded. I headed off out of the gates and up across a bare slope of landfill next to the tip. It smelt pretty pongy round here, but led to fresher fields higher up. Even though it was a much more gradual slope than the one behind our flats, it was quite a distance in the sun and I was soon boiling hot carrying all my stuff. When I got to the edge of the trees I decided I didn't want to lug it all with me. There were beech trees in this part and I tucked my bag in so it was hidden between a tree and the edge of the field, having first put all the food in my pockets. I finished the drink so I didn't have to carry it. Looking back the way I'd come there was just a big expanse of pale gold stubble where the wheat had been cut recently. The hillside stretched away to the horizon and dipped down to the estate on the right. At the far edge of this were the roofs of the school, but the people and playground were out of sight now. It was a relief just to be outdoors, away from the noise, the feelings of boredom and of not belonging.

Here, in the woods and fields was right where I belonged. The trees seemed to stretch out their branches towards me, drawing me in, the opposite of the unfriendliness at school. I patted one of their trunks: it felt smooth, warm and sort of alive, like an animal's body. I ambled slowly upwards, aiming for the clearing I'd been in yesterday. There was the gurgling sound of a stream. The water was just a trickle and I could jump across, but the banks were much wider as if it got quite full sometimes. It wound downhill away from me. Perhaps if I followed its banks upstream I'd get somewhere.

This took me deeper into denser woodland and I couldn't follow its narrow course after a while, so headed off in what I guessed must be roughly the way I'd gone yesterday. By now I was a bit hungry and keen to sit down. Heading uphill, I came to another clearing, but it wasn't the one I'd been in yesterday. This one was full of spanish chestnut trees. I knew them because we used to collect the chestnuts to roast. The trees were easy climbers, with thick, low branches. I selected one that was in the sun and didn't have to climb far to get a comfortable perch.

I settled back and relaxed, feeling the rough bark against my arms. Just like the previous day, all the yuck of the outside world seemed to peel off like dead skin and float away. I ate my biscuits slowly. The branch had a slight bounce to it, it swayed up and down as I held onto the one next to it. Very relaxing, like a cradle or hammock. Folding my blazer under my head I felt like I could almost start to catch up on all the sleep I'd missed the night before. I took off my tie. Perfect. Who would have believed that this brilliant spot was on the edge of that estate? I gazed up into the blueness above. It looked close enough to reach out and touch like the ceiling over my bunks; a bird soared slowly over, hundreds of feet up, reminding me that the blue went on and on forever.

I was bouncing gently in the sunshine, almost drifting off to sleep and humming a little tune. No, it was not me who was humming. Who was then? I opened my eyes and looked around. It seemed to stop. I lay back again. There it went again. This time I didn't open my eyes but listened carefully. It was not exactly a humming sound, more like vibrating. Then it sounded more like chanting, like words. I could pick out sounds like 'viriditi-viriditas.' I had no idea whether these were words or not. But it was quite soothing. It felt as if the sound was coming from the very tree I was lying on. Deep and echoey, slow, but rhythmic. Kind of hypnotic. It didn't worry me. I felt like all I wanted to do was lie there, my body gently rocking on the branch and the sound flowing round and through me. I told myself this wood wasn't where it was: it was somewhere else like near our old farm; and this wasn't now: it was sometime in the past before all the bad things had happened to us. These thoughts grew more and more real and I chilled out till I felt quite spaced and nothing seemed to matter.

∾

I must have slept, because it was much cooler - the sun had almost disappeared. There were many more insects buzzing around, the birds were all busier and preparing for the night. Time to head back home. I wriggled down, stiffer now, but mentally not at all tired.

I could still hear the tune in my head, although it didn't seem real like before. I went forward to retrace my steps. Then realised I wanted to end up at the estate. So I switched direction and carried on in a straight line for a few minutes. Nothing looked familiar. I hurried on through the lengthening shadows, telling myself I would get to a bit I knew any minute now. Then I stopped. I looked around. I leant against a thick trunk to get my breath back. Definitely hadn't been here before. 'Completely lost,' I finally said out loud. Then felt silly, as though someone was watching me. I turned round. There was someone.

How long had she been sitting there? It was the girl from the playground this morning. I tried to look and sound completely cool. 'Do you know the way back to the estate?' She carried on looking at me in that blank way that was beginning to get on my nerves.

'Look,' I said, 'I'm not planning on hanging round here interrupting your privacy any longer than I need to.' (That was diplomatic of me I thought.) 'Just point me in the right direction and I'll be off.'

Finally she stirred herself to speak. 'Close your eyes. Then follow the trees.'

I nearly laughed at her. Exactly which out of the millions of trees around us did she mean?

I could tell she was a strange one, and I wasn't going to bend over backwards to be polite if she couldn't be bothered to help. I marched off at random into the trees, which were full of shadows now. What on earth had she been on about, close my eyes? I tried it for a few moments.

At first, all that happened was that I couldn't see. Then, to my amazement an orangey glow appeared to the right of where I would have been able to see if my eyes had been open. It looked as if a few tree trunks had been lit up by some luminous paint. I opened my eyes and went towards where I'd seen this light. It disappeared when I opened them, so I closed them, and there it was again. I continued walking several paces towards the light and tried to do it here. This time a further set of trees appeared lit up. I walked on and tried the same thing further on; it happened each time. It was as if the trees were guiding me along a route. Well I had nothing to lose by following it as I was already lost.

Eventually after some minutes or so of walking, then stopping to close my eyes, I reached an area that looked a bit familiar. Carrying on this way I got to the clearing I had been in the day before; and from there it was a straightforward downhill trek to the estate.

I felt pretty disorientated as I came back into contact with the outside world again. First, the sound I had heard just before I had drifted off; and now this sort of 'guiding light.'

Was I imagining things? Then I remembered my schoolbag. It was too far to go back and get it now. I'd have to go a bit early on the way to school and collect it then. And try to do my Maths homework before school.

In bed that night I was still thinking about the weird girl, the light in the trees and the sound, that sometimes seemed like a song, sometimes just a vibration. I couldn't get it out of my head. It sounded like 'vi-ri-di-ti'. I reached out for the dictionary on the shelf by my bunk, not really expecting it to come up with anything. But to my surprise there was a word, viridity, meaning, simply, 'greenness, verdancy.' Could that be what I'd heard? It certainly fitted in with my surroundings at the time; and in a way, with the thoughts I'd been having. I'd been thinking how this green forest was more like a home to me, where I felt completely calm and real again, away from school and the estate. Was it possible that my thoughts had made me hear this chanting? It seemed hardly likely, since I didn't know the word before. Nor could the strange lights have been my imagination; without them I could not have found my way home. Perhaps I could look up more about this viridity on the internet later.

These ideas were interrupted by Mum's and Dad's voices next door. Not again. I tried not to hear their arguing. I was just tucking the duvet round my ears as I'd done most nights when I heard Mum say angrily, 'Well someone's got to go to work round here!' Oh no, you shouldn't have said that, Mum. That was like, kicking him when he was down. He didn't reply but slammed off into the bathroom.

I was starting to get really fed up with him. He didn't

seem to want to try to get better. How long would it go on for? Even Lottie had noticed it now. Tonight she had said, 'Daddy doesn't do jokes anymore.' Although she was having more fun at nursery than I was at my school, I wondered how long it would be before she missed having a garden. At least I could take her to the playground like I'd promised. That reminded me about the strange girl from the playground. It felt uncomfortable to think she was lurking around the woods. What could she be doing? Maybe she wondered the same about me.

I realised I'd started, in this short time, to think of them as my woods. If only I could fence a part of it off, just so I'd know there was a bit no one else could go in. You just never knew with someone like that where they'd pop up next. Then I had an idea. My second bright one of the day. I'd make a den! Of course, why hadn't I thought of it before? Somewhere high up in a tree preferably, really secret and tucked away. But I'd have to do it when I was sure she wasn't around. Like schooltime. If she ever went to school. Surely she wouldn't dare take off two days in a row? So tomorrow would be my turn. Especially as I'd not done my Maths homework. I'd get some wood out of that skip; wait till Mum and Lottie had gone of course. It could have sides, and a spyhole, and places to keep my things. I started to get excited about the idea. I'd have to get a hammer and nails without Dad noticing. And some waterproof sheeting for the roof. That could wait till the basic structure was in place, same with the cushions and things. I wondered if I dared forge a sicknote from Mum ... I drifted off to sleep, dreaming of my new house in the trees.

4 Hit on the Head

Next morning I couldn't get in the bathroom because Dad was in there having a shave. This was unusual at this hour. 'What's up?' I asked Mum, who was busy ironing.

'He's got a job interview. At the Council. As a Park Attendant or something. Hardly what he's after, but it's a start. If he gets it. But the letter just came this morning and it's taking place at 9.30 so he's in a bit of a panic. That's why I'm doing this shirt for him. Could you be a huge help and get Lottie ready again?'

'Okay,' I sighed. It was a big day after all, which could affect all of us.

But I hadn't bargained with Dad's sudden burst of cheerfulness once he was dressed and respectable-looking. 'I'll walk with you to school, Louis, it's on my way.' I tried to sound enthusiastic. But it would probably scupper my plans.

He looked as though he had spent his life in a cellar, not on a farm, when we went out into the September early morning sunshine. He seemed kind of surprised to see that the sun still shone out there and blinked like one of our pet owls that used to live in the barn. 'It's going to be a good day, look at the sky,' he said, as though he were off to let out the animals.

I led the way. He did seem a bit happier. Mum had kissed him goodbye before she left with Lottie so things must be okay in that department. He was looking around him as if it was the first time he'd been here. 'No backpack?' he noticed.

'No homework so I left it at school.' I lied. These fibs seemed to flow freely nowadays.

'Oh, alright.' We walked in silence. It was hard to think of what to say after not really talking much for a long time. 'Do you reckon you'll get it?' I asked.

'What? Oh. Who knows? I'm more than qualified for that sort of thing. But it's the kind of job quite a few people might want and there are many more people out of work up here than there are jobs.'

'I bet you're more impressive than all of them though.'

'Thanks.' He smiled for the first time in weeks. I hoped his face wouldn't crack. We were nearly at the school when Farrow and his mates passed. 'Does Daddy walk her to school then?' jeered one of them whose name I did not know.

Dad heard and said,' I'd better say goodbye here then, hadn't I?'

I was relieved and wished him luck. When he was safely out of sight I went into a smashed-up phone box to take stock. I pretended to be phoning though anyone passing would have known I was faking. It stank of wee and cigarettes. I noticed the girl from the playground and the woods. She walked slowly with her head down, like she could barely drag herself to school. But at least I knew now that she'd be safely in school for sure. She didn't see me. It was too good an opportunity to miss. I waited till the last stragglers had gone through the gates then headed quickly and quietly up the hill, hoping no one was looking out of the window. I followed the route I'd taken the night before and found my gear, a bit damp, but okay. Maybe it would be best just to find a good spot today, and get the building stuff later when I knew the coast was clear at home. I made for what looked like the highest point in the woods, a clump of oaks on top of a hill in the distance.

There was a rough track that circled round the base of the hill. After a little while I came to a pile of rocks, very big boulders, granite I thought they were, as they glinted in the sun. I sat down for a bit, my heart thudding with the climb and the worry of getting away from Dad and school. But I soon calmed down. I sniffed the crisp air: it was a good leaf-littery smell, full of autumn and mushrooms. I had already spotted quite a few: the big red and white-spotted fly agarics like something out of one of Lottie's picture books. I wondered if Dad was getting better. If the new pills were actually starting to work. Mum had said the doctor had said they should do soon; but to expect a few ups and downs for a while still. If he got this job it might help, though it had happened sooner than expected and he mightn't be ready for it yet. Maybe all the arguments would stop as well. I turned back towards the town to look at the Council buildings and wish him an extra good luck. To my surprise the town couldn't be seen at all from here; nor could the school. Must have come further round the side of the hill than I'd thought; all I could see was rolling countryside, covered in thick forest, which I didn't remember noticing before. I decided to go on, but how to be sure of finding my way back this time? Maybe I could mark my route in some way. I had no string or anything useful like that in my schoolbag; there was only my Maths book. I loosened the staples in the middle and pulled out a few double pages which didn't make it look too thin. These could be torn up to leave a trail; it was a warm, windless day so that should be fine. I could safely stow all my things in the rocks in that case.

I set off again, lighter, but slightly confused about directions. Still, the paper trail would guide me back. I carefully dropped little scraps every few metres. The track carried on circling the hill, then turned steeply upwards. The thick old oak forest started to thin out and there was plenty of sunshine; in fact it was very warm, like the end of August, when farmers worry about storms and harvests. Surely Dad couldn't have been wrong about the forecast? I hoped not. Certainly it was a great morning and I was extremely glad not to be stuck in a classroom. I took my time, looking around for a good tree, a place I could make my own. I had all day, after all, and meant to make the most of it. Also, the ground was rising now, and though a breeze had started up it was really hot walking uphill. I pulled out the front of my shirt to wipe my face. Then took it off and tied it round my waist. There was no one around, I could have taken all my clothes off if I'd wanted. I felt free and fearless like a wild man of the woods; there were all kinds of rustlings and animal squeaks: birds, squirrels and a few rabbits all seemed very busy, as if they were getting ready for something. Once something bigger bounded through a thicket, probably a deer. I pretended to be hunting for mammoths with a sharp stick I found. Then it seemed to take all my energy just to keep going. The heat increased by the minute; the sky lost its blue brilliance and had a white-hot shimmer. After a while I looked up and found I was practically at the summit of what had turned out to be a very steep hill; and in front of me at the top was the most enormous tree I had ever seen.

An oak, its trunk was about two metres in diameter and too tall for me to see the top from my viewpoint below it. The blinding whiteness of the sky made it hard to look up, too. I stood there, my mouth open with amazement at its size and splendour and my good luck. It was almost like I'd been led there: it was a perfect place for my den. In fact it would be more like a fortress than a den, because I had no idea how I would get up into it; the lower branches were at least twelve feet off the ground. What was also odd about them was the way they stuck out more or less horizontally from the trunk for a few feet before curving upwards. If only it were possible to get up there in the first place, they would make an excellent base for a floor. I couldn't really see beyond the lower branches because they were so thick and leafy and bits of brush and stuff had blown up and caught amongst them. It was starting to get pretty windy up here I noticed, as I craned my head up staring into the heights of the giant oak.

I walked carefully round the base looking for footholds. Unlike the trees I'd climbed earlier, there was absolutely nothing. I would have to come back with some nails and a rope and things. No time like the present. I retraced my steps and looked for the paper trail. It was nowhere to be seen. The wind had really got stronger, and now everything was blowing around quite wildly. Leaves whirled about in the air and the tops of smaller trees swayed in front of scudding white clouds. The animals had all gone quiet and disappeared from sight. The air grew dark and suddenly colder. It was probably going to storm. Maybe I would have to do the den another day. I hesitated, caught between disappointment and feeling a bit anxious. It seemed like I'd better just get home while I could. Hurrying a bit, trying to follow the way I'd come downhill, my tracks seemed to have got covered by the swirling leaves. The wind was blowing all the hot air away and cooling me off rapidly. I turned back up to the giant oak to get my bearings. Had I been past that stump before? I shivered with the drop in temperature. The sun was gone altogether now. I ploughed on, sure I would find something familiar in a minute. But looking up all the time I seemed to have wandered away from the track completely. And once again, I was lost.

I couldn't even get back to the giant oak. I seemed to go round in circles for a while. It doesn't matter, I've got all day, I kept telling myself. But then the rain started. First, just a few large drops here and there; and then it quickly became quite heavy. I struggled back into my shirt as gusts blew it around. But that immediately got soaked. The wind was howling around the hillside now and it was even colder. I tried to shelter in the trees but it was soon so torrential the rain came through and dripped down my neck. In only a few minutes I was soaked through and chilled to the bone.

It was hard to believe that such a bright day had turned into this downpour. For some reason, perhaps because it had become so dark, I started to feel a bit scared. Maybe I was being punished for bunking off. There were all kinds of noises now, not just the wind in the trees, but twigs and small branches being blown off and tumbling to the ground. And a sort of moaning noise that made me shiver even more ... more ... more ... was that a voice I could hear saying 'more'? Then the sound seemed to change to 'fore' ... 'fore' ... 'fore'. I turned round looking for where it was coming from. I was really frightened now, wondering who or what was out there. Suddenly a horror-movie face leered out at me and I yelled with fright. It was an old, twisted trunk with bark gnawed away by deer. Heart hammering, I plunged on past it. Now all the trees started to look quite menacing, as if their twisty black branches would reach down and close around me. I seemed to see faces everywhere: bits of brush like witches' hair and holes in trunks like eyes or gaping mouths. I was completely panic-stricken. Again I heard the words echoing between blasts of wind, and was thinking I could just make out whole phrases, when there was a great bang. My world went spinning into a black hole.

I must have tripped and hit my head and lain there, out of it, for a long time. I became aware of a headache and it all seemed too bright when I opened my eyes. The storm had passed. And so had my unusual panic. I was in a pile of damp leaves at the base of a clump of birch trees. I was a bit damp, but the sun was out again and it wasn't too cold. My clothes were a mess, but drying off. I felt very tired. There seemed to be something soft and furry beneath me: moss at the base of the trees. So this must be the north side of the trees. So home must be in the other direction. But I lay there a bit longer, no longer scared or even too uncomfortable. I wriggled over a few inches so I lay in the full sun. I could almost go back to sleep. But maybe that wasn't a wise idea. I had no idea what time it was. With an effort, I got myself up. I felt dizzy. I leant against the birch trunk in the sun and shut my eyes. All at once an amber glow danced before my shut lids. Of course. The way out. I should have just let myself be guided instead of panicking. I walked slowly forward, stopping every few paces to close my eyes. Again I was guided to where I wanted to be, this time to the boulders where I'd left my things. My bag and coat were still there. But they weren't as I'd left them. The bag was open with stuff half sticking out like someone had been rummaging around and crammed it back all any-how. My pencil case was on the ground. Who could have been here? I checked and everything was there except my comic and snack.

At the edge of the field by the tip I saw school was out and had been for a while as many of the teachers' cars had gone. The bus shelter was empty. Must have been lying on the ground for a while. Better get a move on or everyone at home would wonder where I was. Or would they even notice?

Just as well I got back when I did. Mum and Lottie were home earlier for a change. Mum looked gloomy and all caught-up with something. She didn't notice the state of my clothes or anything luckily. She put her finger to her lips and jerked her head in the direction of their room. 'Dad's having a rest. It didn't go too well, I'm afraid. Not sure what the problem was. I think they talked down to him and he got the huff and wasn't very forthcoming. So he probably didn't get it. It's got him down again, so we'll just leave him to sleep for a bit.'

My heart sank. No prospects of all-round improvements in this family then. 'You look a bit done in yourself,' I noticed, not mentioning that I was too.

'I am. I wish I could just go and have a lie-down like that sometimes.'

'Well do. I'll take Lottie out to the playground for a bit' (Lottie jumped up and down).

'Are you sure? Thanks, I really need it.'

I wasn't just being helpful. Any moment now she would turn round from scrubbing vegetables and ask where on earth I'd been to get into that state, so this was an escape. 'You'd maybe better use Lottie's room to lie in as it's tidier than mine,' I added, suddenly remembering Chanticleer.

We slipped out of the door, both of us eager to be out again. Lottie put one hand in mine; the other clutched a brace of Barbies. 'Do they really have to come with us Lots?' I asked.

'Course. They never been to the swings.'

When we got nearer I saw Farrow and co. were hanging out on the climbing frame, smoking. Lottie ran ahead and started to climb up. 'Get out of it kid, this is our patch,' snarled Farrow's pal, a larger, meaner looking version of him. Lottie's mouth fell open; she'd never been talked to like that in her life before.

'Why?' I demanded angrily. 'We've got as much right as you to use this stuff!'

'Don't talk no rights to us, new girl. This is our patch I told yer, we was 'ere first, piss off.'

The knock on the head I had had earlier seemed to have left me irritable and not thinking very smartly. I said furiously, 'You going to make me?' For an answer, he lurched out from one of the bars, his feet level with my head and launched his large boots at my head. For the second time that day I ended up on the ground.

'Yeah!' he said, having jumped down now to tower over me.

Seeing red, I socked him a massive punch I hadn't known I had in me, and winded him. He was bent in two, and I thought I'd beaten him, when the other two swung down like orang-utans and set upon me kicking and hitting me. I was no match for all of them. Lottie started wailing. 'Come on!,' I gasped, grabbing her hand and we ran, her howling all the way like she was the one who'd got beaten up. 'Let's just get home again,' I panted. The gang didn't bother chasing us luckily, they just slouched there laughing. I was stupid to have hit back, it was so predictable what happened, but I'd just had enough of them.

Back home, before I could stop her, Lottie burst in on Mum and woke her up. 'Louis has been hurt very bad Mummy!' Mum came stumbling out of my room.

'Who on earth did that?' As I told her she bathed my face and cleaned up a cut at the side of my mouth. I had started shaking a bit, realising it could have been a lot worse. Then she made tea. She was quiet during the meal.

I had an early night. I didn't see anything of Dad. Mum came in to say good night. 'How are you feeling now?'

'Got quite a headache.' I said, although I suspected this had more to do with my fall in the woods.

'I think you'd better have a day off tomorrow,' she said, 'I'll write you a note.' I agreed quickly, thinking that would come in useful for today as well.

'Oh and by the way, I lay down in here as Lottie's room was too much of a tip ... and Louis, that bird's got to go.' Silence. What could I say? I was secretly amazed she didn't have more of a go about me keeping Chanticleer. Maybe she realised I'd had enough for one day, though she didn't know the half of it. Or maybe she privately sympathised about keeping him.

'I could see if there are any local poultry farms in the phone book -' she started to say.

'It's okay, I'll sort it Mum.' I said with as much firmness as I could manage. She looked relieved. One less thing to do, no doubt.

'Good lad. Good night then. Sleep in, you may as well. And just leave Dad to himself tomorrow. He'll - he'll come right in his own time,' she said, trying to sound sure. She reached up to my bunk to hug me. 'That's better. I've hardly had time for you I've been so preoccupied.'

I didn't say anything. I didn't say it didn't matter, because it did. She had hardly spoken to me about my new school, and had only shown concern for me when I got beaten up. All her attention was on her new job, on managing Lottie, and dealing with Dad's moods. She didn't need to bother about me because good old Lou could always be relied on. I wondered how much longer I would put up with it. Maybe I'd get a bit less reliable. Or at any rate, please myself more from now on. But all I said was 'goodnight.' There was the immediate problem of Chanticleer to deal with.

5 A Rapid Recovery

The next morning I did not get much of a sleep in; I was woken by frantic scrabbling, under the bed and what sounded like a half-throttled 'cockadoodle-do!' Mum was right, of course, he would have be kept somewhere else. I was anxious Dad might have heard. He would not react as calmly as Mum. My whole face seemed to throb and the previous evening came back to me. I got up and checked out the flat; a half-eaten bowl of weetabix on the table, the spills hardening to concrete; clothes thrown about the living room, all signs of the usual morning rush from Mum and Lottie. Dad's door was still closed, though, so I crossed my fingers that he was still asleep. I'd better get Chanticleer out as quickly as I could then, in case he did wake. But where? I went to the bathroom while I thought about it.

I got a shock looking in the mirror. There was a huge bruise round one eye, and a vicious looking scab forming on my mouth. It hurt to do my teeth so I didn't bother. My last waking thoughts about doing what I wanted came back to me.

Okay, so I'd do something about Chanticleer. Something acceptable to myself and to him. A strange farmer would take one look at him and offer me next to nothing (I'd seen it happen when we left the farm); or worse still, demand to know where he came from and call the police. At best he'd end up in someone's oven. I thought and thought; my head still hurt a bit and thinking seemed to make it hurt more.

There was the pet shop down the road. But they probably wouldn't call a rooster a pet. It looked like it had been shut for some time anyway. He really needed somewhere he could scratch about in the fresh air and crow without attracting attention. I opened the bathroom window. You could see the tree tops high on the hill from this side of the flats; they were really close in fact. That was kind of comforting. What about taking Chanticleer somewhere in the woods? Would he be safe? What about foxes and so on, I wondered?

Then, looking out again, I realised this steep side of the wood looked familiar; the rounded hillside rose very sharply to a peak crowned by one tree that stood out from the rest. I had a feeling, I was sure I was right, that it was where I'd been yesterday before all my plans to build a den had been wrecked by the weather. Very odd, I hadn't known at the time that I'd been so close to home when I got so lost. I must have taken a very long route back. I was going to have to get a proper, detailed map of this place, like those large-scale ones that show every farm-building on them. But I'd need some money first. And for now, I could see exactly where I wanted to get to: back to the giant oak. If I could rig up a den there, perhaps I could keep Chanticleer there overnight and go up each day to give him a run around.

I felt a bit better now I had a plan. I threw on some clothes and grabbed half a loaf for later to eat in my new den, when I'd got safely out of the flat.

But it wasn't going to be that easy, getting all the stuff I needed as well as Chanticleer, up to the top of that hill. For a start, I needed a rope and didn't have one. Hammer and nails I found in the laundry. The only thing I could see, which would have to do, was a very long, orange extension cable. It would be strong, for sure, but might get a bit wrecked; but when were we going to need it to trim hedges or mow lawns again? It also weighed a ton when it came to carrying it with everything else.

In the end I settled for two trips. I'd leave Chanticleer in the basement bin shed for a short time, to get him out of the flat before Dad woke; meanwhile I'd go up with the things and make sure I could get into the tree and that it would do for him.

This all took longer than expected. Chanticleer was in a strange mood when I pulled back the cover and peered into his box. It was in a really bad state, stinking and pecked to bits with feathers and bird poo everywhere. I felt guilty. It was nearly as bad as battery hens. All I'd wanted to do was to save him. 'Come on then, I'll make it up to you, you'll feel like you're in a palace up there,' I coaxed, to try to get him out. But he just jerked up his head and hopped out of reach, fluttering his clipped wings. It was as if he didn't trust me any more. Then he opened his beak and started trying to find his voice again, although it didn't come out properly. I had to act quickly. I pulled off the cover from my duvet and spread it with the opening wide apart; as soon as he stepped into it

I pulled up the sides, bundled him up protesting and struggling, and rushed out of the flat and down the stairs. He was a big, heavy bird and wasn't exactly cooperative, but I got him down, and stowed him in the basement bin shed together with old pushchairs, bottles and newspapers. I pushed some of the stacks of paper around him to make a rough pen, and opened the duvet enough for him to breathe; then closed the doors and hoped for the best. I went back to the flat for the other things. Luckily there was still no sound from Dad.

I lugged the den-building equipment up the hill as quickly as I could. Passing the clearing I'd first discovered, I kept going uphill in the same direction. Soon I reached a small cliff a few metres high where some of the side of the hill had come away, and there was a steep wall of soil with tree roots sticking out of it. I was sweating with my efforts by now and my head was really throbbing. Somehow I had to get beyond this to reach my goal. Looking for a way up either side of the cliff it seemed useless; there were thick trees and solid walls of bushes.

Dropping down again a short way, I tried branching off to the left, circling the hill, very aware that I did not want to get lost again. In the end I got to a clearer part and was able to climb slowly through the woods and up to the summit and the giant oak.

It turned out as I would have expected, that I was approaching the tree from a different direction to the day before. It looked no easier to get up. But there was no time to worry about difficulties, I would just have to get on with it.

I unwound some of the orange cable and threw up the

plug end as far as possible over the lowest branch. It just made it. As it was a bit stiffer than a rope it could be pushed up and further over, I hoped. I bent down to unwind some more from the reel. Then something hard hit me on the head. Not again. It was the plug from the cable, which now lay on the ground again. I didn't think I'd pulled on it at all. So I threw it up again, this time with more flex behind it. It went over properly this time with a good few feet hanging down the other side to keep it there. I moved over to pull some more over. Just as I reached out to the plug, it shot up in the air and the whole thing lay at my feet again. I couldn't believe it. I had another go and the same thing happened. What on earth was going on? I didn't have time to waste like this, with Chanticleer waiting to be rehoused or discovered.

I decided to try another approach. I got the hammer and nails to make some footholds. About to drive the first nail in, I heard a shout: 'No!' and a white face appeared in the lower branches.

It was the girl from the playground. Not again, I thought. She seemed to appear wherever I wanted to be. But I was in no mood to be messed about like this.

'You're in my den!' I shouted.

'Oh yes, so you've been coming here for some time have you?' she replied. There was no answer to this, and no point arguing about it either. She continued.' At least since yesterday?' Then she threw something down. It was my comic. 'Have this back, it's boring and childish. And go away and leave me alone. I've been coming here for years and I don't need company.'

I might have known. That such a perfect place would already be taken. I'd have to find somewhere else for me and Chanticleer. I picked up the stuff I'd brought and the comic, turned on my heel and made my way back down.

It had been exhausting getting up there, and now disappointment added to this, my headache, and the problem of Chanticleer.

I found my way back to the other clearing and sat down in a patch of sunshine. I pulled off a chunk of bread and chewed on it while wondering what to do. The situation with Chanticleer was even more urgent now I had moved him to where anyone might come across him. Why did life have to get so difficult all the time? I lay down for a moment, feeling done in. I closed my eyes, bright light still hurt; my head ached and my mouth was sore. I knew what a sight I looked too, I wondered what the girl had made of that. Probably thought I was the sort who went in for fights ... I tried to calm my swirling thoughts. I took long breaths of the fresh forest air and drank in the greenery. I did what I'd done the day before and imagined I wasn't here but back on our farm or somewhere nice; and that all this hadn't happened; I was back in a time when life was easy, and my face was smooth and unharmed. As I pictured it, it seemed to throb ever so slightly less; I started to feel a bit more relaxed and very soon, was drifting off somewhere. I must have slept.

In my sleep I was back at the giant oak. Dreaming, but it seemed so real I could hardly believe it was a dream. It was one of those dreams where you say to yourself, "I know I'm having a dream; if I pinch myself I'll wake up". Or, as I usually do, carry on enjoying it anyway, knowing it's a dream. That was what I did then, as it was so interesting. Gone was the hostile pinched face of the girl from school, and gone was all my exhaustion. Instead, there was a crowd of people in old-fashioned long clothes, probably Tudor, but they were sort of peasanty so it was hard to tell. They were laughing and drinking, and singing, and playing old musical instruments. There were so many of them: men, women and children. And when I looked up, I saw the most amazing thing: an enormous platform built across the lower branches of the tree acting as a dance floor. People were whirling about, clapping and singing, it was surprising they didn't fall off.

The whole thing was decorated with strands of ivy and white flowers. A boy in a green tunic with boots and what looked like tights offered me a drink of some sweet stuff, and I found I was singing as well: a tune I hadn't heard before but seemed to know now. Then a dark-haired girl in a red and blue dress came by, grabbed my hand and whirled me off into the dancing crowd. I was surprised to find I could do it as I'd never learnt to dance before. I pushed aside the curtain of hair that hid her face; it was the girl from the wood, but she was laughing. After a while it seemed as if her skin was all green and her face was part of a tree trunk, a young sapling. And so was my own. In fact all the people in the dance were trees with human faces and expressions. I felt vital and alive, feeling the sap flowing through my branches, turning my face and leaves to the sun, which filled me with energy and strength.

∽

I woke up feeling calm. In fact, better than I had felt all day. No longer concerned about the den and its owner, about Chanticleer, home, or the fight the day before. There was a new kind of ease and lightness as I strolled back down through the trees. Outside the flats I met Mum and Lottie coming home; Lottie rushed up and threw her arms round my waist. Mum started to say, 'I thought you were resting ...' then stopped and looked at me, puzzled. 'Your face is almost better, hardly a scratch.' I put my tongue out to my lips as I had been doing all day, sort of worrying at the scab. It did now feel very nearly smooth.

'That's so weird ... I do feel better in fact.'

'It's practically healed up! How wonderful.' Gently she touched the side of my face, as if to feel where the scratches had been. 'How could that have happened? What have you been doing with yourself all day?'

'Just lying around really. And then I went to get a bit of fresh air up the hill there. I lay in the sun and dozed off a bit ...' I trailed off, confused.

'Well it's obviously done you some good.'

Lottie was hopping about restlessly. 'I want to go up the hill.' I thought for a moment, remembering how yesterday's outing was such a disaster, and said to Mum,

'Can we? Just for half an hour before tea?'

Mum glanced at the trees. 'Well don't go too far. But yes, if you're up to it.'

We didn't go far. But there was no need, Lottie was excited just to be somewhere a bit green; she'd not been in any proper outdoor spaces since we moved. She found flowers and snails and I helped her climb some very low branches of a pine tree. Then we went in for tea. Dad still wasn't about, but I decided just to enjoy the new calm that had come over me and not worry about him and Mum for a change. After dinner I got out the three-day-old Maths homework and did it easily. It was only much later when I was getting into bed that I remembered Chanticleer.

I had obviously gone too laid back. How could I have forgotten him? All those blows to the head must have done my brain in. Mum was still up, preparing some work for the next day. I didn't want to get her involved in case she insisted on doing something I didn't want. I would have to wait till she'd gone to bed and sneak down. I lay awake for what seemed like hours, but she just didn't go. In the end I fell asleep.

6 Chanticleer Disappears

But I woke first thing, knowing I had to both deal with Chanticleer and put in an appearance at school. I waited till Mum and Lottie had left the front way. Dad was about, I'd heard him go to the bathroom, but he was not out and dressed yet. Grabbing my school stuff, I rushed downstairs. I opened the inside door at the top of the steps and went down into the basement. The outside door to the back yard was wide open, and swinging in the wind. Chanticleer was gone. The duvet cover was still there, full of feathers and poo. I looked out the back and all around the yard and garages. He could not have got the back door open. Someone must have opened it. He had completely disappeared.

I looked everywhere I could think of. Not a sign. Could he have been taken by someone? I cursed myself as I hurried along the road, I didn't care about being late, or getting told off for it by Mr Simon. If only I had taken better care of him.

'And where were you the last two days?' Mr. Simon demanded. I practically threw the absence note on his desk without a word. He opened it, glanced at it, and in turn threw it to one side. Expectations were pretty low all round here it seemed. I slumped into my seat, hardly hearing the lessons. I noticed the girl from the woods was in my class - it was the first time we had both been in school at once. But we avoided each others' eyes.

At break, I slipped off to the library to get away from everyone, and went on the internet for something to do. Searching for trees and dancing I came up with a lot of interesting stuff that for the moment took my mind off Chanticleer.

For instance, it turned out that platforms really were built in large trees for dancing on; they trained the branches to grow out horizontally to provide the floor base. It seemed amazing to me that I should dream about something I'd not even known about.

I discovered more as I read. There were stories about trees themselves dancing and moving about generally: whole forests could go on the march or get reshuffled, and this was thought to happen particularly when the world was out of sorts; or there was some threat to the way of life in the forest. This was all a bit weird for me, and I was about to go back to lessons when another bit caught my eye:

The ancient forest was the source of viriditas, or green life-energy; it could absorb bad things from the environment and purify those who came through it. It was also known as a place of healing, for mending physical ailments or healing psychic distress.

I thought about my healed face and feeling of calm after my sleep yesterday in the woods; Mum had said it was like a miracle to see it completely better in so short a time. Was it possible just being in the woods had healed it?

As I went back to class Farrow jostled me and said: 'See we've hardly damaged your pretty face then new girlie. Mustn't be so gentle next time.'

I kept well away from them and all the boys at lunchtime just in case. I pulled out a book and sat near the cycle shed with my head in it hoping not to attract attention. I was just getting stuck into it when I heard what sounded like a yelp from the shed. I opened the door. There were four older girls standing round someone smaller. Then I saw it was the girl from the woods.

'Witch's babe! witch's babe!' they taunted, kicking and slapping at her. A large red-haired girl had a pair of scissors and was lifting up the girl's long dark hair. 'What a slut! this is filthy witch's hair. Needs a good haircut don't you think girls?'

I rushed in before I had decided what to do. I thought quickly: they outnumbered me and were all much bigger even if they were girls. I'd be no match for them. Besides, I was sick of fights. So I yelled, 'Mr. Simon's coming! Get out quick!' and took advantage of their surprise to grab the girl's wrist and pull her out into the playground. We ran for the school building just as the bell went. I could feel her shaking. Then I remembered her unfriendliness to me in the woods and was about to leave her to sit down, when she muttered: 'Thanks. Meet you up at the tree after school?' I stared, then shrugged.

The teacher came in and we had to go to our separate places. At afternoon break she had disappeared - bunked off I guessed. A pudgy boy called Mervyn came up to me with a secretive kind of smile on his face. 'Saw you sock it to Farrow's mate the other day. Nice one. No chance with three of 'em though.'

'How d'you see?' I glared.

'Out me winder. I'm in Swaller court ain't I?'

'Oh. Could've given me a hand then couldn't you?'

He laughed disbelievingly. 'No chance. Not worth messing with that lot. Anyway, Mum had me tea ready and Simpsons was just startin.' I turned away scornfully, but he carried on.

'Yeah, they're bad news them three. Do all kinds of crime on the estate. And another thing, that Fern Woodruff is a weird one. Saw you together at lunchtime. I wouldn't get involved with her if I was you.'

'Why?' I was curious even though I didn't want to get involved with Mervyn.

'They say her Mum's a witch.'

I sneered. 'Don't be stupid!'

'It's a fact. She wore all these weird clothes and had really wild hair. And she used to make all these kind of potions. But she ran off with some bloke anyway, a few weeks ago. Reckon Fern's funny like 'er too. You want to be careful ... You can come and watch a horror movie round my place after school if you want' he added suddenly.

Two invitations in one day! 'I'm busy this afternoon' I said quickly, and then the bell went.

It didn't take Mervyn to tell me this girl Fern was weird, I had already spotted that for myself. But witchcraft? Then I remembered her telling me to follow the trees, and the strange guiding light. Well, if she was a witch, it would be better to keep on the right side of her. Maybe she could tell me where

Chanticleer had been taken. I was a bit intrigued now, and most of all, wanted to know how she got into the giant oak. If she'd tell me. I decided to go and meet her; at least it was a genuine excuse not to go round to Mervyn's. I reckoned we did not have much in common apart from hating Farrow. I left my backpack at school. This time I really didn't have any homework, and tramped up past the tip to the fields and the woods. I decided not to go home first just in case I got held up by anything there, and to take the longer but easier route over the field to the summit of the woods.

7 A Den in the Wood

Fern was waiting up in the tree already. 'Hold on, I'm coming down.' She disappeared from amongst the branches, appearing a moment later from behind the tree.

'How do you do that?'

'Come round. Look.' Near the roots, in a deep pile of leaves, a board covered in bark, like a rough trapdoor, lay to one side. There was an upside-down v-shaped hole at the base of the trunk which it had obviously camouflaged. The tree was hollow inside. 'Come on up. There are footholds inside. I'll shine the torch.' She went ahead. She had changed her tune a lot since we last met up here. It was quite easy to get up once you could see the footholds. She shone the torch down from above, waiting patiently.

I came out into daylight and was gobsmacked. 'It's fantastic!' It was all I had imagined for a den and more. A flash of jealousy went through me for a moment, which then turned into curiosity. 'Did you do all this?'

She nodded. 'It's taken a while though. I've built it up over the years, starting with just a few boards.' There was a good-sized floor made of planks tied to the horizontal branches;

it was well hidden from below by the thickness of the lower branches and the leaves and brushwood I'd assumed had just blown up there. Now I saw they were cleverly arranged to hide the floor and the rest of the hideout. A natural seat was formed by a curve in one of the thick branches as it grew upward from the horizontal; another was made out of a low wooden box with an old cushion on it. A longer box on its side held a number of useful things; a coiled rope, a pile of books, a blanket, torch, a biscuit tin, an oil lamp and a small gaz camping stove. It's perfect,' I sighed.

'Thanks. Would you like a drink?' She got out a bottle of water. I found the two biscuits I'd been about to eat after lunch when I'd heard the noise in the bike shed. 'Are you okay now after lunchtime?' I remembered to ask. It seemed like a long time ago up here.

'What? Oh, them, yes, fine.' Her face clouded slightly but her tone was light. 'But thanks for coming to the rescue.'

'What was it all about?'

'Oh, they're just nasty pieces of work.' She changed the subject. 'Look, sorry I was a bit off yesterday. But it was a bit of a shock to find someone strange in the woods, then trying to get into my tree; it's been my secret place for so long, you know, and I thought you were like all the rest at first; they're real idiots some of them.'

'Telling me.' I could not have agreed more. 'You don't go in that much, do you?'

'I just can't stand it sometimes. Most of the time. And the work is so boring; I was at a proper school before this.'

'I've never been to any other school before. Aren't they all like this then?'

'No way. Our family can't afford it any more now, but my last one was really cool. I had friends, even the teachers were nice, mostly. You didn't have a uniform and there was no fighting or bullying. They made the lessons interesting too. Here, well, you've seen it. They can't keep order half the time. So how come you've never been to school before?' I explained about home-schooling.

'So your Mum taught you at home?' She sounded quite envious.

'Yeah, she made it really fun. We didn't just sit and do bookwork all the time; we were outside just as much, doing experiments or collecting nature things. She's a Spanish teacher so she taught me that by helping me email my cousins in Spain. Or we went on trips for some subjects like history to different towns and museums and things...' Suddenly I could hardly bear to talk about it, it was such a contrast to now, and I missed it so much.

'There's quite a good museum in town, surprising considering what a dump the rest of the place is,' she said kindly, watching me. 'I used to go there a fair bit when I was at my other school. It's got lots of fossils, and some not bad history bits.' I could see she could see I was upset; but I wasn't ready to let her know how I felt about everything yet.

'Oh yeah? How do you get to it then?'

'On the bus. Same one I take to school, it goes on into town. Number Seven.'

'Do you live a long way out then?'

'No, just the other side of the wood. Wheeler's Farm. It's

not that far if you walk directly over the fields round the edge of the wood. It's much longer by road. But sometimes I'm late or it's pouring ... but it's good to save up the bus fares too. Also some of the people that catch the bus to school can be a bit, you know ...'

I nodded. We ate our biscuits in a kind of comfortable silence. I started to feel more okay with her. There wasn't anything particularly witchy about her, except her long black hair and pointed nose. Her strange green eyes were quite nice really when she smiled, which wasn't often. She seemed fairly normal after all, just a bit of a misfit at school maybe, but then who was I to talk? I caught her looking at me.

'We're a bit similar, you and I,' she said. Had she read my thoughts?

'Um...maybe. So what kind of farm do you have?'

'Mixed. Organic. A few hens, ducks and geese, but crops, mainly, specialised. My mother made herbal remedies and aromatherapy stuff which she sold, and she grew everything for it herself. A lot was mail order and Dad took care of that side of the business ... he can't really keep it all up by himself though.' It was her turn to look upset, and she turned away.

'I heard your mother's -' not around, I was going to say, but before I could finish she snapped,

'What? What did you hear? That she's a witch? That she ran off with someone? It's not true!' To my alarm she burst into tears.

'I didn't say I thought she was. I'm sorry.' I offered her a crumpled but clean bit of loo paper.

She dabbed at her eyes and blew her nose. 'It's okay. Well

it's not. It's really, really awful.' She started crying again. I looked up into the branches. After a while she stopped. 'I didn't mean to do this. But Mum's disappeared. It's bad enough not knowing where she is, whether she's dead or alive; but all the gossip makes it even worse. Dad got a letter a little while after she'd gone. It was meant to be from her. It said she'd had enough of being unappreciated and was going to live with someone who did appreciate her. He doesn't know whether to believe it or not. It was typed, in this funny font, not by our computer. I know it wasn't written by her. She just wouldn't do that to us. Sometimes she used to moan about having too much to do, but mostly she was happy. She loved her work and definitely loved us too.'

Before she could start crying again I asked, 'But didn't anyone try to find her?'

'At first there were a lot of searches everywhere. But after that letter the police gave up. They said it was just a domestic situation between husband and wife and there was nothing they could do. They weren't exactly fond of my mother anyway.'

'Why not?'

'Because she was involved in all these protests about the wood. She made their life really difficult. This wood used to belong to our farm. We had to sell it, we were short of money. The Council bought it to use as a Recreation Area; they'd been looking for something like it for a while as there's no decent open spaces round this town where people can go at weekends; they were just going to put up a few signposts and information boards, maybe a picnic area at the bottom.

I would rather it had been left as it was of course, but it was a million times better than what happened next; the person behind the idea left the Council before it was listed as Rec. Area, and this real idiot took over, and sold it to a developer of a theme park! There was no consultation or anything, it happened behind our backs. You should see what they're planning: cutting down almost all of the trees, using this hill for a roller coaster - it's just awful. So Mum and her friends had this camp where the road comes by the wood, with banners and stuff; and whenever anyone from the theme park company came out to survey it they made a huge racket banging saucepans and everything, and generally getting in their way so they couldn't make a start. It went on for months. Dad was really for it; though he didn't join the camp as someone had to keep the farm going or we would have run out of money like we're heading for now. After a while most of the women had to go back to their families and get on with their work too. But Mum just stayed on, patrolling the edges everyday, making a big nuisance of herself whenever anyone came and tried to do anything. I was, like, really proud of her. She was so tough, refusing to give up. They tried getting in the police, who couldn't do anything. But they got pretty fed up with being called out there in all weathers. And so I think they were a bit relieved when she disappeared.'

'Whew.' I thought for a few moments. 'Don't you think the developers had something to do with her disappearance?'

'Of course they did. It's obvious isn't it? But everyone is saying she was a weirdo and ran off with someone, because it suits them. The police at least,' she added bitterly.

'Have you kept on looking yourselves?'

'Of course. Dad and I have been all over the countryside. We've put posters up in town and in the villages; you'll probably see a few old ones and some that have been mucked up. Many were ripped down though. People generally were a bit suspicious of her round here; because she's a bit different, I guess - into alternative stuff, doesn't dress from M and S, you know. And a lot of them really want the theme park. They're bored. They don't know what to do with themselves. We've looked just about everywhere. But without the police behind us it's very hard; people think we're kidding ourselves about her as we don't want to think she's run off and left us. They laugh at Dad behind his back. It makes me mad. But I know she wouldn't do a thing like that. So does Dad most of the time. Only now he's starting to get quite down and wonder if they're right and he wasn't seeing how she really felt. I think he's afraid, too, that she may not be alive still. I know she is; I don't know how, but I do know.But I don't know where to look next!' She buried her head in her hands.

'That's so awful. I thought my situation was bad; it's like having only one parent most of the time ... but at least I know where both of mine are. This is the worst nightmare I can imagine happening to anyone.'

She looked up then, gazing bleakly at me. After a while she said, 'You're the first person my age who really understands, I think. It's why I don't talk to anyone at school anymore.'

'It's not hard to imagine how bad it would feel, say, if my Mum went off somewhere.'

'The worst thing is not knowing. And feeling so stuck, not

knowing what to do now.'

'What's her name? Your Mum?'

'Beth. She reached into the cupboard and pulled out a thin plastic bag. Inside was a photo in a frame. It was of a group of laughing, hippy-looking women in brightly coloured clothes holding hands in front of a tall fence covered in bits of ribbon and pictures and stuff. 'That's her,' she pointed, 'at Greenham.'

'Greenham Common?' I vaguely remembered hearing about the women's camp around the American airbase at Greenham Common; they had been protesting against the cruise missiles in it and nuclear weapons in general.

'Yeah. And yeah, she does make a habit of this kind of stuff. But I'm proud of her. Someone's got to save the planet.'

'For sure. And what about all this?' I looked at the den, the tree, the woods in general.

'It'll go. It's just a matter of time. Of course, I'm gutted. But compared with not knowing where she is, well, it's not the same scale of things is it?'

'No.' But I was gutted now. This wild wood, this one bright bit in my life, was soon to disappear too. When Fern told me what had happened to her mother, I felt guilty for feeling fed up about my own life. But now I was fed up again; just as an escape had appeared in the shape of the wood, it was to be snatched away. The sun was sinking low and orange.

Fern said 'I've got to go. But come up here anytime while it's still here. Make sure you put the bark cover up at the bottom when you leave and don't bang any nails in.' She was down the hollow trunk and off before I could ask what that was about.

8 The Healing Wood

My mind was whirling as I plunged slowly down the steep slope that led to the back of our flats. The route was more familiar now; but I was not seeing my surroundings. I was seeing the den in the giant oak, and Fern, with her pale serious face talking, telling the whole awful tale of her mother and these woods, that had not ended yet. Sometime in the not too distant future, none of this might be here. The trees that had guided me, that seemed at times to sing to me and maybe heal me, they could all be felled. Or killed seemed a better word; they were living things, almost like people. I wondered if Fern thought this too; she must do. Her mother would have done; that must be why she'd resisted so bravely - until? until what exactly had happened, I wondered? Fern's situation was unbearable; no wonder she seemed withdrawn and suspicious. But she had opened up to me in the end, and invited me to share her den while it lasted. I didn't know if I would have been that generous if it had been mine. She deserved some friendship and support. I was determined to at least try to find out what had happened to her mother; even if it was something awful, it was better to know than not knowing. The obvious people to check out would be her enemies: the developers. I had no idea how to find out who they were. It seemed hard to believe no one had really looked into this seriously already.

But as I reached the back of the flats my speculations were suddenly cut short.

'Oy - you! that your bird in the shed?'

'Where? where is he?'

'Gone thank christ! bloody menace, flew right in me face, nearly pecked me eyes out! It's illegal, keepin' poultry, and in communal areas, an' I've called the council they're comin' round straight away.'

'But where's he gone?' I shouted desperately. The man standing in front of me was beefy and red-faced, with his hands on his hips. I recognised him as the man who had been renovating the flat with the skip outside. I couldn't believe Chanticleer had been seen, and was now lost again.

'Flew off thataway.' He pointed towards the way I had just come. 'An'good bloody riddance!' I didn't bother mentioning that Chanticleer couldn't fly. I dashed back the way I had come, scanning the ground uselessly for clues. All I could find was a tiny plastic Barbie shoe about as big as my thumbnail. I returned round the front of the flats to avoid the skip man and think what to do next.

No sooner was I in the front entrance than I bumped into Dad, who also started bombarding me with questions. 'Where've you been? where's Lottie? Is she with you? I can't find her anywhere. Mum's not back is she?'

'Dad - stop. I don't know anything. What's going on?'

'Lottie's gone. I was looking after her while Mum went back into town for some things; the Council rang me - I was only on the phone five minutes and when I turned round she'd gone! I can't find her anywhere.' He was sweating and hoarse with worry. I showed him the little Barbie shoe.

'I found this. Don't know if she dropped it today or the other day when we went to the woods, but we can look where I found it, see if there's anything else ...' Together we rushed down the stairs and out of the back door to the yard, ignoring the stares of the skip man. I made for the spot where I'd found the shoe. There wasn't anything else. Then I remembered how Lottie had liked climbing the low trees nearby. 'Let's look up there.' I suggested. There was something - a flimsy little bit of brightly coloured nylon that was obviously some other bit of Barbie clothing. But no Lottie. I shifted my gaze up at the hillside.

''Could she have gone on up there?' asked Dad doubtfully. He seemed quite helpless with worry.

'Let's look,' I said, more confidently than I felt. We climbed the steep slope together, and at the top we were rewarded by a hairband I knew was Lottie's. I was glad of her habit of scattering her belongings everywhere she went right then. Then, on some loose earth, there were small sandal prints. These quickly disappeared, but had given us a pointer for which direction to try. We made our way much further to the other edge of the wood than I'd been before.

Then the trail seemed to run cold. There were no more clues and we now had no idea if we were on the right track or not. Dad was despairing. 'How could she have got so far in such a short time? And why on earth did she want to come out here? Or did someone take her here?' He moaned. "Sally will never forgive me. Half an hour she left us and I couldn't even keep her safe for that short time.' He was really having a go at himself now, like it was all his fault. He never thought like that before he got this illness.

'Shush Dad! Just concentrate, you might miss something.' We seemed to be descending a bit, and weren't that far from a road as I could hear the occasional car. Oh no, I hoped Dad hadn't thought what I'd thought. Lottie wasn't very good with roads yet. 'Let's stop and think a minute,' I said. We stood there, staring at each other and the silent woods. And then,

'Cockadoodle-doo!'. A loud, clear, unmistakeable Chanticleer-like crowing filled the air. We both jumped. It came from a little copse a bit further on. I set off in the direction of the sound.

'Why do you want to follow that? It's not her,' said Dad. But I had to somehow. He followed me reluctantly. We heard the sound again, twice. Ten minutes later we came to a clearing. And there, in the middle, with a serene smile on her face, sat Lottie, surrounded by Barbie gear and Chanticleer. Dad rushed across and grabbed her to him so tightly I thought he'd squeeze the breath out of her. Then it was my turn. I tried to be a bit gentler, but I was shaking and trying not to cry.

'Be careful, you'll mess up my head-dress' said Lottie haughtily. In her hair were several small feathers from Chanticleer, who seemed to have been moulting. He was strutting about, also looking haughty, and pretty much like his old self.

"Why did you come here Lots?' I asked, when I could speak.

'Well, you see,' she began importantly. 'I lost my Barbie's shoe and Daddy was busy on the phone so I went down to find it myself. Then I found these feathers and they made a good Indian head-dress for Barbie and me, and I wanted to go and play in the woods where you took me, Louis. Then I found Shonty and he kept flying farer and farer away and I thought I better get him home. And then he stopped here, so I did too, I like it here.' She had no idea what we had been through.

Well, let's get you home.' said Dad. But we didn't move. Lottie carried on playing, occasionally tugging at my arm to show me something. Chanticleer scratched about, apparently completely restored except for his missing feathers. Discovering him had been overshadowed by finding Lottie, but I was quietly delighted. Although anxious too, as I was back to square one in terms of what to do with him. I lay down in the soft grass to try and think. Dad lay down too, and closed his eyes. We both kept an ear out for Lottie's chatter and opened our eyes if it paused, to check she was still there. We seemed to need to rest and were incapable of moving. Chanticleer scratched quietly at the soil beside me. It was still warm and gold bits of sun glinted through the turning leaves. Birds chirruped softly as they settled down for the night. It brought back memories of the paddock at our old place. After a long while Dad stretched and said, 'It's good here, isn't it?'

'Yeah.'

'Feels better with a bit of greenery and trees. That looks

just like our old rooster.'

'Mm.'

'It *is* Shonty,' said Lottie.

'Lottie and I came up near here before,' I told him, changing the subject. 'She really liked it.'

'Maybe we could all come, with a picnic,' said Dad. 'I really like it too. There's no reason to stick around the flat all the time ... oh and the Council phoned when you were out -'

'A picnic!' shouted Lottie, who was obviously getting hungry. 'Let's go home and get a picnic and bring it back here!' I was glad she got him off the subject of the Council and Chanticleer, but was surprised he hadn't put two and two together after seeing his own rooster out here and getting what was presumably a complaint about him. 'I want a picnic now!' she shouted again.

'It's getting late now Lots. Let's go home and make a list of what we want to bring another day.' said Dad surprisingly swiftly. He stretched and started to sit up. I wondered what to do about Chanticleer.

'I might go down to the road and see if any buses come this way - it's only through there,' I said. I had no idea what I could do still, but thought it might be easier to get Chanticleer back by road, somehow. I followed the direction I had heard cars going by.

There was a clearing by the road and in fact, a bus stop for the number Seven. But according to the timetable the last bus had gone. I looked around for inspiration. I noticed the area had been cleared and a freshly made four-wheel drive truck led into the woods here from the road. A number of trees had been cut down and lay around in the churned up soil, their leaves shriveled and wilted. I felt something shrivel inside me. It must have begun. The beginning of the end of the wood.

I walked heavily along the road a few metres. Around the corner there was a portacabin which said 'Private Property Keep Out.' Next to it was an area of cleared woodland, surrounded by a high steel fence. Inside it had all sorts of gear for construction and clearing: fencing, rolled up wire netting, fluorescent red plastic ribbon by the mile; and a whole stack of notices saying 'Danger - Keep Out'. There was a bulldozer and what looked like a tank armed with chainsaws. I shuddered. I was just about to go back to the others when an old rusty pick-up came rattling along the road and stopped suddenly next to me. I expected a security guard to jump out but it was Fern who did. Always turning up at odd times; but not unwelcome this time.

'Haven't you got home yet? It's been hours,' she asked, surprised.

'Yes, I've been home - but we had a bit of a crisis - lost my little sister and just found her again out here ...'

'Oh dear. Dad - this is Louis. He's new at the school, in my class.'

'Hi there,' said a pleasant but sad-looking man. Want a lift?'

'Oh no, it's okay thanks ... but I do have another problem.' It suddenly occurred to me that maybe they could help with Chanticleer and I quickly outlined my difficulties, missing out much of the saga.

'It's no problem,' said Mr. Woodruff. 'We've got hens, no other roosters at present, and plenty of space. I'll take him.' He moved the truck off the road and got out.

I couldn't believe my luck for a change.

We walked back to Lottie and Dad together. I noticed Fern stared straight ahead as we passed the excavated area. We were just leaving it for the trees when I saw bits of ribbon that were not fluorescent plastic, but small coloured scraps of cloth, tied to a tree. I didn't think now was the time to mention it but made a mental note of it. I didn't want anything at all to hold up Chanticleer's rehousing.

Dad and Lottie were surprised to see the others. I introduced them and explained they were taking the rooster, as I called him for now. Dad looked even more surprised. 'Well, good, yes.' Lottie started to say, 'but Shonty's ours' and Fern quickly offered,

'You can come to the farm and visit him if you like.' That was sufficiently exciting to keep her happy and Mr. Woodruff carried Chanticleer under one arm down to his pickup. Dad and I thanked the Woodruffs and made our way home, having promised Lottie we'd visit.

Dad seemed quite bemused by the whole thing. 'It looked just like our old rooster,' he said. I thought then, at last Chanticleer was safe, so I might as well be honest. I told him the whole story, even about keeping him under the bunk. When I got to that bit, he started to laugh. It was a strange sound. We had not heard it for so long. It seemed so odd, Lottie started to laugh too, and then I did, more out of relief, I suppose, that a) we'd found Lottie, b) I'd found Chanticleer c) I'd at last got him a new home d) Dad wasn't cross and e) I realised he seemed happy. I would not hold my breath; he'd shown signs of improving before which had come to nothing. But tonight there was definitely something different about him. It seemed like he knew it too.

'You don't give up, do you, Lou? Not like the rest of us. Or myself to be precise. But I feel like I could be on the mend; funny thing, but something seemed to change up in the woods. After we'd found Lottie and we were lying on the grass, you were humming a little tune, and this really soothing feeling crept over me, almost like I'd just swallowed a wonderful new medicine that acted instantly. But better, because it was natural.' This was the longest speech Dad had made since we'd moved. I didn't say I hadn't been humming anything. Instead I said,

'I've felt better, too, whenever I've been in the wood. My face had nearly healed up after only a few hours there. It's as though there's something special in the woods, almost like they make you feel well again.'

Mum was quietly delighted by the change in Dad, which didn't stop when he got back to the flat. He helped her un-pack the shopping and bathed Lottie, and chatted just like his old self. Or more than his old self in fact, as he'd never been that talkative before. When he got to the bit about Chanti-cleer, their eyes met, as if to say, 'boys.' I thought to myself, if I'd had someone there to catch their eyes, we'd be thinking, 'parents!' but then I recalled my duvet cover, a detail I hadn't bothered to mention and thought they might not find it so amusing if it got ruined; I slipped downstairs to get it and hide it till I could deal with it.

Mum had made a big paella for tea while we were out - everyone's favourite, with profiteroles for pudding. 'I thought I'd do double quantities and freeze half so you can just reheat it one day when I'm working late,' she said. But we were so hungry we wolfed down the lot.

We were just finishing when Dad said, 'I've just remembered, The Council phoned -' Oh no, I thought, this'll spoil things,

'and I've got the job!'

'Tom that's fantastic!' Mum exclaimed.

'Dad! Why didn't you say before!' I laughed, again relieved.

'Good boy Daddy!' said Lottie and everyone laughed.

'I kept trying to tell you, but so much was happening that I kept forgetting,' he explained, looking pleased.

'Well, tell us all about it,' said Mum.

'It starts this Monday, and it's a bit better than Park Attendant. Apparently they've had another unexpected vacancy. I'm to oversee all the municipal parks and 'small green spaces'. That means things like the roundabout they've planted up towards the motorway; or those raised flowerbeds in the pedestrian precinct. I don't have to do all the work - someone else helps with mowing and trimming and so on but I have to make sure it gets done. There are bits of basic maintenance too, all quite straightforward I should think after the farm. And a few meetings apparently; don't really look forward to those or see the point of them, but apparently it's par for the course nowadays.'

'Yes it is.' Mum agreed. 'No one seems to escape those.'

'There's just one potential problem.'

'What's that?' Mum asked.

'The job was offered on the condition I had satisfactory health clearance. I don't know if my illness will count against me.'

'We'll go down to Dr. Williams tomorrow and let him see how well you are for himself; I can get back earlier tomorrow if you can look after Lottie, Louis?'

'Sure.'

That night as I drifted off to sleep the snatches of conversation were quiet and happy. Mum was saying, 'You must have made a better impression than you thought.'

'Lou encouraged me on the way in.' (I wriggled proudly under the covers though I knew it was not me that was responsible for his success.)

'He's really together with all this going on, isn't he?' Mum commented. (Yeah, well someone's got to be.) 'Except for smuggling in Chanticleer - but all's well that ends well ... You know, Tom, you're so different, even from this morning. What's changed, was it getting the job?'

'No, because the minute I'd heard about it, I realised Lottie was gone and didn't have a second to think about it. I honestly forgot about it till later; and I didn't feel better until we were in the woods, just lying on the grass, Lou and I, while Lottie played ... I was thinking about how lucky I was to have you and our two... but that wasn't all of it ... I don't know. It was the place. Just being there. A kind of peace seeped into my bones; and I knew I was getting better, without a doubt. I know I've had temporary improvements before but this one's real, I just know it. Then there was a lull in the conversation and some scuffly sound as if they were cuddling - yuck. So I pulled up the coverless duvet round my ears as usual and went to sleep easily.

9 Fern's Farm

School was not too bad the next day; Fern had condescended to come in and we had Biology which we both liked, and we shared a microscope. It was only looking at sections of plant stems - xylem and phloem, that sort of thing, but she knew masses about it, as much as the teacher I wouldn't have been surprised, and I got really into it, staining the sections, then drawing all the intricate patterns of cells.

Of course we drew a few comments - 'got yourself a girl-friend, new girlie?' - the usual stuff; but before I knew it the morning had gone and I realised I had actually enjoyed school for the first time. We stuck around together at lunch as well, 'in case you get hassled again' I said, wary about admitting I liked being with her.

'I'm not really worried about them,' she said defiantly. 'They're always picking on younger kids, they get bored easily, and move on to someone else.' I noticed, however, that her hair was freshly washed and tightly plaited today, as if to keep it out of harm's way.

'How's Chanticleer settling in? You and your Dad saved my life by the way, taking him in. I'd have been well and truly stuck.'

'He's fine, strutting about like he owns the place. Why don't you come round and see him tonight? Bring Lottie.'

So later that afternoon when Mum and Dad went down to the surgery, Lottie and I boarded the bus down at the estate shops, and headed out for Wheeler's Farm. The bus driver raised an eyebrow when I said where I wanted the fare to. I asked him to tell us when we got there.

Lottie was excited. 'Can I keep the tickets?' She gazed out of the window, commenting on everything we passed. Most of the people from school had already gone by an earlier bus except for one boy who must have had a music lesson as he carried a strange-shaped black case.

The driver didn't bother to tell us where to get off; but I recognised the stop from Fern's description. 'Over the white river bridge there's a lane on the right opposite the stop.' We then had a half mile or so to walk up the lane that was signposted Wheeler's Farm. The whole journey the bus had made had skirted the woods on the hills to the right; they were various heights and distances from the road, but always there, making me realise they occupied a very large area even though the road had wound about a lot. About halfway on the bus route we'd passed the cleared area where I'd met Fern and her Dad the night before.

The river, as we crossed it, was a good size; not so huge as to be dangerous for swimming or anything, but a big enough size to do things with, and clean-looking and not too deep. We leant over the white rails of the bridge and could see the bottom only a metre or so away, with long green weeds streaming straight in the current.

'Look! there's a fish!' whispered Lottie. So there was: in fact half a dozen, about two inches long. I showed her how to play pooh-sticks with a couple of long leaves and she was really chuffed when hers won.

'We'd better go and see if Shonty's okay now.' I said. But thought how this place would be a great place for the summer … that was, if it was still here. There was a small field between the river and the wood here and I wasn't sure if this part was included in the woodland that had been sold.

After about five-hundred metres we rounded a bend and saw the lichen-covered rooftops of Wheeler's Farm, which had been hidden by trees from the road. It was in a sort of valley at the bottom of the wooded slopes and with a patch of woodland shielding it from the road. Small fields and little greenhouses stretched behind into the valley. It was a very private little place. Or not so little; apart from the main farmhouse, there were lots of outbuildings and barns.

We could see the wood smoke we'd smelt coming up the lane rising straight up in the cool, windless air; it was a kind of picture book farmhouse and I almost expected a rosy-cheeked farmer's wife to come out welcoming us with a cream tea ready. But I knew Fern and her Dad were on their own. Besides, even at our farm it hadn't exactly been like that; Mum had always been really busy with the business side of things, looking after Lottie, teaching me and her evening class, while Dad did the practical stuff. I felt a lump in my throat thinking of it all again, so was glad of Lottie to distract me. 'Look, there's ducks and geese!' she cried. There were, lots of them, gliding dreamily, almost gloomily it seemed to me, over the surface of the murky pond. Our geese would have been up and honking at strangers, but this lot seemed in a world of their own. It was incredibly mucky near the pond, more so than the usual farmhouse duck pond, with a solid carpet of goose poo and feathers, so I steered Lottie away and over to the house.

This had once been really nice, but now looked a bit neglected: wisteria had got into the roof and the windows; old wooden trellises hung off the walls, held on only by the creepers. The crumbly red bricks glowed in the late afternoon sun and there were a few chrysanths along the edge of the house. All the paintwork was really old and peeling. But I didn't mind these things – I thought the place perfect as soon as I saw it. Just as we reached the front door, Fern came out. 'Hi, thought I heard voices. Want to come and see him then?' She addressed Lottie, who nodded, wide-eyed.

She led the way round the back to the barns and outhouses. There was a huge sort of kitchen garden behind the house with normal things like tomatoes, then rows and rows of herbs, most of which I didn't know, though there were some I did, like chives and thyme. The air was full of their smells and I breathed in deeply. The beds were hedged with lavender which had finished flowering but had silvery-grey-green leaves which I crushed a few of in my hand as I walked. 'Good for the nerves!' Fern laughed, noticing. Then her face fell as she seemed to think of something and she went quiet. 'I want some,' said Lottie, and Fern came to and broke off a bit of oregano for her. 'Delicious,' Lottie said and carried on plucking at everything until I stopped her. We were walking along a little path of old red bricks the same colour as the house; at the end of it, Fern pushed aside a wooden gate that had come off its hinges, and we were in a yard with hens. They were just pecking about like hens do, and some seemed to be getting ready for the night, clucking their way into an old henhouse that needed mending.

'Do you get many foxes?' I asked casually. Fern nodded, looking worried. 'Yeah, and we're asking for it at the moment. But Dad just doesn't get time to fix everything, and I'm not very good with tools and stuff.'

'I could come and do a bit on the henhouse here if you like,' I offered, anxious for Chanticleer's safety. I had been going to volunteer Dad, then thought it might all remind him too much of his own place, like it did me in fact.

'So could I,' said Lottie helpfully.

Fern smiled. 'Okay, thanks. We've got all the equipment you'll need. But it'll have to be in exchange for Chanticleer's bed and board. Can't pay you, you know.'

'I *know* that,' I said, cross that she should even think of it. 'But maybe check with your Dad if he wants me to do it.'

'Oh no, he'll be glad of the help I'm sure.' It was getting near to the time of the last bus back, so Lottie and I said goodbye; it was hard to tear her away, and I arranged to come straight after school the next day to do the work.

10 Chanticleer's Battle

I didn't see much of Fern at school the next day as we were in different groups. She had Food Tech. which she hated, and I had Construction which I would have enjoyed, except not with the people I was put with. There were three other guys in my group and they kept drilling holes in the work bench, threatening to drill each other and making it impossible to do anything. I was glad when it was the end of the day.

Fern and I got on the bus at the school gates getting plenty of stares and comments. We made for the back as it was a bit quieter there. She seemed more down than the day before. 'A fox got in already. But he only managed to injure one of the hens - it's got a broken wing and a lot of feathers missing. There are millions of feathers everywhere, there seems to have been a fight. I didn't hear a thing in the night. I think Chanticleer gave as good as he got; he looked a bit ruffled this morning and there were bits of orange fluff stuck in his neck feathers, and his comb is slightly torn, but he's okay really.' I hated to think what a near thing it must have been, though I felt proud of Chanticleer.

'Don't worry, we'll get it all fixed up, really secure.' But she still looked a bit gloomy so I asked if anything else had happened.

'No. It's just all ... such a struggle, one thing after another since Mum disappeared. She turned her head away and looked out of the window.

'Fern, I want to help you with that too. Just let me try.' When she turned back her eyes were teary but had a look of surprise in them.

'What could you do that we've not tried already?'

'I don't know, I don't know. But we can't just give up, can we?' She looked bleak at that idea for a moment, then agreed firmly, 'No.'

'So let's get on with it' I said, trying to sound upbeat. We were at our stop and got off and made our way in silence up her lane. At the farm, we went straight out to the hens together. She showed me a shed where there were tools and chicken wire, then went back inside. I found the place the fox had got in and mended it, although I was surprised to notice the holes looked more like they'd been cut with something; there were a few other dodgy bits, but these didn't take long. It was something I'd been used to doing for some time at our old place. Then I went to find Fern.

She was sitting at the kitchen table, a nice old pine one a bit like the one we used to have, with a pile of what looked like bills in front of her. She looked really worried. 'Dad hasn't been paying these for some time. I'm worried about him, Louis, he's not coping. I think he's got that thing ...'

'Depression?'

'Yeah.'

'Yeah, I know a bit about that.' I told her about Dad and she listened silently. I said how he was a bit better now.

'Dad wouldn't go near a doctor, let alone antidepressant pills. He and Mum only liked alternative remedies. And she's the only person he'd ever listen to for health things.' She put her head onto her hands with her elbows on the table. After a few moments I said, 'I don't have any more idea how to find her than anyone else just yet. But maybe I need to know more about her. About her work, her interests, friends, that sort of thing. Isn't that what private detectives do first, build up, like, a picture of the person?'

She looked doubtful. 'I suppose I could show you her study. Dad's a bit funny about that. But he's out delivering to health food shops at the moment so we've got a bit of time. Only you mustn't touch anything.'

'Of course not.'

'Oh, and, before I do, you should see this.' She reached into a drawer full of more bits of paper and pulled out a typed letter. 'This was what Mum was supposed to have sent to Dad.' In a strange font I'd not seen before, the letter just said she had had enough and was going off with someone who did appreciate her.

'Why would she bother typing it if it was just to your Dad?'

'Indeed. Someone didn't want their handwriting to be identified is what I think. I'll show you her room now.'

She led me into a stone-flagged corridor and past a sitting-room with saggy couches and an old piano in it; then past a couple of rooms which seemed to be used as storerooms, full of boxes and little bubble-wrapped packages; then at the end of the corridor she opened a door which led to a room with windows on three sides; it was a light, airy room with views over the kitchen garden one way, the lane the opposite way, and across a lawn to some small cottages and beyond them to the fields.

'Who lives out there?'

'No one now; they were farm workers' cottages, but we had to let the people go recently. There were two young guys and a family:, they each had one of the cottages.'

I looked inside the room now. It was amazing. What must at one time have been perhaps a posh drawing room was now a cross between an artist's studio and a laboratory. Every inch of wallspace was covered with charts: herbal remedies, different medicinal plants and also lots of Celtic stuff: poems, songs, pictures of knots and crosses. There were also pictures of trees and photos of gatherings. One of Stonehenge I recognised, but with a lot of people presumably at some solstice celebration; and then there were the tables and benches. It was hard to move around the room, they took up so much space. An old mahogany counter with brass-handled drawers under it held coloured bottles and plant bits preserved in what looked like oil; there were test tubes with dried up bits of plants in them and old-fashioned weights and scales. And books, everywhere. Thick ones with faded gold writing, half falling apart, and a lot of files, next to piles of papers and letters. It was all so busy and messy-looking it was hard to believe someone wasn't going to rush in and say 'Get out of my hair, I've got work to do.' I was already imagining Fern's mother just from the one photo I'd seen and her study here, but maybe I wasn't on the right track at all. 'It's ... cool. How much time did she spend here?'

'A lot, before the business with the woods. Most of her time, when she wasn't outside checking on her plants. Sometimes late into the night. But she always got up to see me off to school. Once the protests started she didn't come here much. She used this place mainly to research new and old remedies and try new ways of preserving them. Dad dealt with all the commercial side, and still does; though he doesn't know how to mix and prepare the remedies, he's just using up stocks that are left. He says we're running out of a number of things and customers are getting impatient.'

'But she was also into other stuff, wasn't she? All this Celtic stuff.'

'Yeah - she was into alternative healing more generally; and she got a lot of ideas from Celtic things I think. As well as just liking its symbols, and the art. She did these paintings ...' She showed me some weird colourful kind of abstracts with a lot of symbols scattered in them. They weren't horrible or anything, but I didn't understand them. I could see how Beth might have got a reputation for witchcraft, though I didn't of course say this.

'What do these lines mean?'

'I don't know. Oh, I think they're from the Ogham alphabet, based on trees. She's a bit nuts about trees you know.'

'Same here.'

'Oh, yeah. You've heard them, haven't you?'

'What? Well, some things, sounds ... songs, sort of?'

"Mm. And they helped you find the way out?'

'Yeah, more than once. And, maybe, healed my face when I got beaten up. I think they might have fixed my Dad's mood too, touch wood.'

'See. We say 'touch wood': when we touch wood we're safe, we're healthy; when we're in touch with the wood things go okay in the world; when we're out of touch with the wood everything starts going wrong. The wood knows, you know ... it's not just xylem and phloem and bark; there are things it picks up and gives out to us, to keep us safe. But only if we take care of it too - which right now is not happening. In the old days in some places if you damaged certain sacred trees you could be put to death.'

I gulped. 'Is that why you stopped me banging nails in?'

'Yeah. A tree feels things, too.'

I sighed. I felt no nearer my goal, just like I was beginning to realise how little I knew about certain things. I picked up a small, more modern-looking paperback about trees and leafed through it. 'This looks useful ...' thinking it was time I started to understand a bit more.

'I should think you could borrow that for a bit if you want; it's not one of her special books,' Fern replied.

'Thanks. Are you going up to the wood this weekend?'

'If only. I've got my cousin's wedding so we're away the whole weekend. I'm not looking forward to it. All those concerned relatives. One of them even offered to come and keep house for me and Dad! Luckily he felt the same way as me. But no, I can't go up there. But like I said, feel free to use it yourself.'

'I will, thanks. What I'd like more than anything would be just to go and chill out there, read things like this book and so on. I feel like I need some space to think about everything. Maybe we can talk more when you're back.'

'That would be good. You've given me fresh hope. See you Monday. At the tree after school?'

Now I felt very responsible. I had been so concerned to keep her spirits up, to keep her from giving up, that I hadn't, silly as it now seemed, stopped to consider how realistic this would be. What had I taken on? But someone had to.

11 Duir

On Saturday Mum and Dad decided we would all go into town. As a family. Trying to act like a normal family at last, I thought, a bit cheesed off as I'd wanted to go up to Fern's den. But I went along with it as they were being quite nice and happy for a change. Also there might be stuff I wanted.

We had a little bit of money to spend now Dad had his job; or at least, they were spending it expecting his first pay packet. He hadn't actually earned anything yet. We took the bus in, a short ride from the shops on the estate, and got off in the High Street. We all needed bits of clothing, and things looked like getting heavy again when Mum wanted to go to Debenhams and Dad said, 'Why pay all that money, when you can get really good stuff for a fraction of the price in Oxfam?' In the end, Mum took Lottie off for some new shoes and Dad and I browsed around Oxfam. He picked up a brand new pair of leather boots for a fiver and was well pleased with himself. Even Mum was impressed when we showed her later. I wasn't really interested in clothes shopping, but got stuck into all the old books and stuff. There was a whole heap of camping gear, sleeping bags, little stoves and so on. I started thinking to myself, wouldn't it be cool if I could spend a night up in the tree. Then Dad was calling me over. 'What do you think of this jacket? Mum says you need a warm one with winter coming on.'

'Maybe. But not one like that.'

'Okay. Well have a look yourself at those others then.'

I couldn't see anything I could imagine myself in. Then a brightly coloured top caught my eye. It was a woman's, a sort of tunic with coloured ribbons threaded through, that looked somehow familiar...where had I seen something like those before?. Of course, the fence the developers had put up at their entrance to the wood. There had been a few ribbons just like these tied to it. I lifted the tunic down. Sure enough, around the bottom there were some ribbons missing, apparently deliberately snipped off, leaving the background material, a purple woven fabric with flecks of red in it. Could this have been Beth's? And what was it doing in Oxfam? I shivered suddenly.

Dad noticed. 'Not quite you, I don't think. Or even Mum. Let's go and see how they're getting on before they buy too much.' I was glad to get out, feeling suddenly repelled by all the second-hand clothes and their mysterious memories.

It was a relief to sit in a cafe eating ice cream with Lottie and looking at all their new, unworn clothes. Lottie was over the moon about some stripey tights and Mum had bought me a new winter jacket that was warm, fitted and reasonably okay-looking, so that was a relief.

Dad had a little map of the town showing the main places of interest. 'I think we've almost done them all ... High Street, war memorial, riverside walk, museum ... what about that?'

I remembered Fern mentioning the museum and said I'd like to have a look.

It was in what had been a Victorian school. One room had been done out like an old schoolroom, with little wooden desks with lids that lifted up, and inkwells, and slates for writing on. Lottie was a bit freaked at first by the lifesize model of a schoolteacher standing by the blackboard, chalk in one hand, cane in the other; but then she got completely into it and didn't want to leave. She sat at a desk, drawing on a slate, talking to herself. Mum and Dad went and looked at an exhibition of old farming tools and I saw a sad look come into Dad's eyes. I left them to it and found the nature bit. There were the usual stuffed animals and wooden drawers full of butterflies, and then there was, as Fern had said, a really good collection of fossils. There were ammonites, trilobites, belemnites and plant fossils like horsetails and ferns. Above the display cases, on the wall behind, there was a local map showing where they had been found. To my surprise I saw that a lot had come from the area of our estate and the woods. Then I noticed the year most of them were found: 1965. The other day at the entrance to the estate I had come across a battered old sign saying that Kingsmead had been officially opened by the mayor of this town in 1966. So probably the fossils were found as they dug the foundations for the flats. Interesting. I wondered if there were any left still. You'd need a pneumatic drill though, to get through all that concrete to find out. Except for the part at the edge of the woods. A map of the woods was just what I'd been looking for. Disappointingly, it didn't cover all of them, only a few hundred metres or so beyond where the estate now was and then it was the edge of the map. The estate wasn't marked, so it must be a fairly old map. The contour lines were very close together at one point - that must be the steep bank behind Oaklands that I had climbed. Then I noticed right at the edge of the sheet, further back in the woods, a funny little symbol like an old castle. I looked at the key: 'Ancient monument/fort/burial place.' Cool. That would be worth taking a look at. But which of those things could it be? I was pretty certain it wouldn't be a complete ancient monument, I'd surely have come across that by now. But there were masses of mounds and humps that could be something. I wondered who might know more about it. I'd seen a woman sitting in the museum shop; maybe she'd be able to help.

I found her rearranging and polishing souvenirs that were for sale, very quickly and nervously with a little cloth she kept flicking. She didn't turn round when I came and waited, even when I coughed gently. So in the end I said, 'Excuse me.' Then she turned suddenly and looked at me, never stopping fiddling with her duster. She was middle-aged, with long hair held back by a Celtic-looking clasp and an anxious-bird kind of face. Her large glasses flashed as she nodded, 'Yes?'

I asked about the symbol on the map and she dropped her cloth suddenly and bent to pick it up. When she resurfaced she looked even more flustered. 'That's a very out of date map, and it's not accurate. They may at one time have thought there was some sort of settlement up there but that idea has been discredited. The area has never been used for human habitation - it's too steep and inaccessible.' She laughed nervously and turned back to her fiddling. What a funny woman, I thought. And why work in a place like this if you don't like talking to the public? She left the counter to go inside a door marked 'private.' It was then that I noticed her skirt. The same purply material as the top in Oxfam! It was quite unusual. I had nothing to lose and felt a bit bolder somehow because of her nervousness, and said, before she could disappear, 'I like your skirt.' This was guaranteed to cause further flappiness of course. She went red in the face, then said, 'Thank you. It used to be part of a suit actually.' Then she scuttled out.

So. At least it wasn't Beth's. But could this twittery, birdy woman have been involved in the protests in the woods? It seemed unlikely. I had to go back there, and find out more about the developers. I'd take another look at those ribbons on the fence. I was also dying to go and sit in the den and do some reading. Even though I liked Fern, the idea of having her den to myself for a bit was extremely appealing. I thought I would take the bus out toward Wheeler's Farm that afternoon, and get off at the site entrance where I'd met Fern and her father; see what I could find out while there was no one working there on a Saturday, then walk back the way Dad and I had trailed Lottie and on up to the giant oak for a read.

But on the way home Dad said, 'What about that picnic we promised Lottie? How about later this afternoon?' I sighed quietly. When was I going to make the most of the den on my own?

Mum said, 'Great idea. We'll take a rug and a few games

for Lottie ... you can play with her or take a book or something, Lou, I've got a bit of marking I can do up there.' The bus was crowded and Lottie started whining as she was hungry and tired from the long morning, so I didn't say anything. I did not want to mention the den.

We had a quick lunch, and packed up ready to go out again. Lottie's mood did not improve even after she had eaten. Mum started wondering if she was well. She looked very pink.

'Maybe it's not such a good idea; she could be coming down with something. Maybe just you and Dad should go, Lou.'

'No!' shouted Lottie so furiously none of us dared suggest it again. 'She's probably exhausted after the long days at nursery,' said Dad. 'But just as well she's got that now.' Mum looked at him and smiled. There'd been an argument about spending money on the nursery place. We set off, through the yard, the way Dad and I had gone when we looked for her. We needed to go the least steep way because of Lottie, but also I wanted to steer them away from the den.

Lottie grizzled all the way, saying she was tired and demanding to be carried. Dad put her on his shoulders and she still kicked and complained. We got to the clearing where we had found her and Chanticleer and when he set her down she was bright red in the face and seemed to have a temperature. But she rushed around madly, demanding to climb trees with me. I had more or less written off the day though I had brought a book in case.

It was no better climbing with her. She kept slithering down, hurting herself and crying. Not the relaxing outing we'd had in mind. In the end, thinking about the den still, I said, 'Let's make a house here Lots.' I could see a good spot at the base of some pine trees, which only needed one or two branches to enclose with a wall.

This helped, and she said, 'But where's the bedroom going to be?' Mum and Dad had slumped down on the grass with their eyes shut, a bit exhausted by then and hadn't got the rug out, so I took it and made her a sort of nest in the house. She quickly snuggled up in it, put her thumb in her mouth and kind of fingered her Barbies like she does when she's going to sleep at home; within a minute she was fast asleep with bright red cheeks and shining forehead. Dad was snoring and Mum's mouth was slightly open.

Looking around I realised that no one was going to miss me. I could go off for a while and do some of the things I'd planned after all.

I made my way down to the road where I'd met Fern and her Dad the other night, and went to look again at the construction site.

I was surprised to find a lorry there and a couple of men unloading more fencing. I sat on a tree trunk that had been cut down and watched. After a while they finished and stopped to have a break. One of them said 'Hi' to me in a friendly way and offered me a bit of chewing gum. I asked what all the stuff was for.

'This lot? Kind of theme park for disabled people.'

'Disabled?' I was surprised.

'Yeah. The boss has a handicapped daughter and is really keen on doing things for disabled people.'

This did not quite fit with the picture I had of the developers. 'Would there be a lot of money in it?'

'Dunno. Probably not. But he's not doing it for money - he's got plenty already. It's more, like, his pet project.'

'Oh.' I tried another angle. 'Weren't some of the locals against it?'

'Yeah, didn't want to lose the wood and an' all that. He weren't too bothered by the protests, said he'd just bide his time, and sure enough it's all died down now.'

'You don't think he'd want to get rid of any of the protesters - you know, have them locked up, or like, threaten them if they didn't shut up?'

'Who, Alf?' Both men laughed their heads off at that idea. 'Not him. He wouldn't hurt a fly.' They seemed so truly amused by this notion that I realised I was probably barking up the wrong tree. And they didn't even work for him, they were just doing a delivery. I'd have to think again. I said goodbye and turned off into the woods. At first I followed the little track I'd come on with Dad. I wasn't taking much in; I was thinking about Beth, and the odd woman at the museum; they might have known each other. Maybe the museum woman knew something that would help me shed some light on what might have happened to Beth. But I couldn't for one minute see her answering any questions. She'd been shifty enough about ancient settlements. Why? I wondered. I found it hard to believe her answer about maps not being right. I thought the people who made maps did these things really carefully. But why would she want to deny anything was there? Maybe she just didn't want to talk to schoolboys. I would just have to look for the settlement - monument, fort, or whatever it was, by myself. I left the track and headed up the steep hill, in the general direction of the giant oak but varying it a bit from previous trips in case I could uncover anything new.

I couldn't. It was a nice walk, the new way I'd come, skirting the steep hill very gradually in the autumn sun, without any obstacles. But I didn't find any evidence of forts or stuff like that. At last I puffed up the remaining steep slope to the summit with the giant oak. I was approaching from a completely new direction this time, and looking back I could just see the rooftops of Wheeler's Farm in the distance. This must be Fern's normal way back from school when she didn't take the bus, I reckoned.

The oak stood splendid as ever, its great branches thrust out then curving up like a giant figure with many arms outstretched and bent at the elbows. It looked so powerful and yet so sheltering. At last I could do what I'd imagined doing for so long - curl up in a tree den with a book by myself.

Carefully I removed the bark door from the base of the tree. I'd remembered a torch but with the sun out today I didn't need it; there was just enough light to see the footholds.

I pulled myself up and climbed out into the den. It was as perfect as I'd remembered it. I put my backpack down and helped myself to the cushions, which I stacked against the trunk. Now I was more than ready for the snack and water I'd packed. I ate and drank slowly, just sitting there, taking in my surroundings. I'd got out the book Fern had lent me, meaning to read it, but for now I just wanted to relax and enjoy being there. Branches, leaves and sky could look amazing with a little sunlight and a light breeze to lift the leaves. I sighed. This was perfection. What made it all the more magical was how private it was and knowing no one would come and interrupt me or even see me. I was invisible from below. Only the birds knew I was there. It no longer mattered that it was Fern's place; because she had said I could come here on my own, and in any case, she was alright to have around, not bad at all for a girl. I wouldn't have minded some of my old friends like Dylan and Josh, but they probably wouldn't have stopped talking.

What was so perfect here was the quiet; just the breeze in the leaves and the occasional birdsong. I fell into a sort of trance just lying there, gazing up at the sky through the lit-up flickering leaves. My body felt weightless on the cushions. I was very warm after the climb and the sun was directly on me, so I took off the thick new jacket Mum had bought that morning and put it over me like a blanket, and carried on doing nothing. I only had a t-shirt on underneath and in a while my arms grew cooler so I stuck them through the sleeves in front of me. I closed my eyes.

A deep voice said, 'About time you divested.' I was startled, I'd thought I was completely alone; and yet, I realised, I'd all along felt someone or something else was nearby.

'Where are you?'

'Under you. Holding you. All around you,' said the voice. It had a pleasant, deep, resonant quality to it.

'Who are you?'

'I am Duir, the strong oak. And you are Louis, the rowan, the birdcatcher, green and newly sprouted, only just divested.'

'What does that mean?' I was astonished, but not afraid.

'Well you just reversed your normal mode of donning your garments did you not?'

'Yes ... I suppose.' I had put my jacket on back to front if that's what this Duir was talking about.

'So now you are completely open to our spirit.'

'So putting on my clothes back to front means I can receive your messages?' I didn't think talking was quite the right word for what I was taking in somehow.

'Quite so.'

'Does this happen with everyone?'

'By no means. Only a few who are receptive to our spirit.'

'What is your spirit?' I asked, although I could guess.

'It is a thing you cannot see or touch, but is all around and inside you; and is there between trees and people and between people and other things ... it has many names. Some call it viriditas, the green spirit of creation, but it takes many forms. You may feel it in the song of a bird, a poem, a strong harmonious community, a green place or a fertile garden. Sometimes it is not there at all, and sometimes it is threatened, and may be extinguished.'

'I think I know what you mean ... it's here in the woods, isn't it?'

'Of course,' boomed Duir.

'But not on the estate ... or at school?'

'There it has been destroyed. And that is why you are here; these are bad times and we need new young saplings to regenerate the spirit. But first you need to be replenished yourself, and that is also our role: to sustain and protect you, succour and revive. It is a difficult life you are living now.'

'How do you know about that?'

'It is a knowledge we have gathered over thousands of years; one that may not be put into words, but contains all that is happening everywhere, all that has happened ... and, not always happily, things that are going to come to pass.'

'Can you see into the future then?'

'We feel rough shapes of things to come ... which we cannot speak of but can only sense and be vigilant to defend against ... and now you must sleep.' I immediately felt very drowsy. I hoped nothing too awful was going to happen, then became aware of some sounds that were like music but nothing I had ever heard before. Then a low voice began to sing (was it Duir's?) It sounded a bit different this time:

When Duir comes to the king
Then shall cease all manner of thing
The evil dwelling shall be consumed
The poisoned land entombed
by thunderbolt and lightning flame
viriditas once more shall reign.

What could all this mean? But I was too sleepy to wonder for long; I finally drifted off then, if I hadn't been before.

∾

When I came to, it was cooler, so I put my jacket on the right way round without thinking any more about it and tidied everything away. I climbed down and carefully replaced the bark door, and piled a few leaves around. Then I went back down the slope. As I stumbled, still a bit sleepy, through the thick autumn leaves, fragments of the words I had heard in the tree came back to me. Did I really hear these things or did I dream them? They had sounded quite real at the time, but then so do dreams. The last ones had been like some kind of prophecy; I got the feeling that something big and dramatic was going to happen.

Slowly, I made my way back to the others, still wondering about it all.

Mum was still asleep. Dad was awake, but lying on the ground watching Lottie. She had woken up and was pottering about singing to herself and picking flowers and putting them in the house. I stared at her in surprise. She was completely better.

12 Strange Events at Wheeler's Farm

Monday was Dad's first day at his new job. We walked together as far as the shops on the estate where his bus took him into town. I told him more about Fern and her mother's disappearance. I considered telling him about my strange experiences in the trees, but thought better of it.

Like I had been, Dad was shocked. 'But they can't just stop looking for someone like that ... I suppose it comes down to manpower in the end ... the police have only got so many officers to do so many things.'

I told him a bit about Lottie and I going to Wheeler's Farm and how nice it was after the estate, but how run down it had become. I even mentioned how it made me think of our old place. 'I really, really miss it Dad. I know you and Mum do too. Only, now I know about Fern, I know there's worse things than losing your house.' He had been back to his tough old self ever since the day Lottie got lost and I thought it might do him good to remember other people felt things too.

'That's dead right, Lou,' he agreed. We'd reached the bus stop. I wished him luck and trudged on to school. I felt very slightly grumpy this morning; I was glad my parents were happyish again, but I wouldn't have minded them asking after me and my new school (not that I wanted to think about it when I didn't have to, let alone talk about it), just to show an interest.

Today, having had all weekend away from the place, the contrast with the autumn woods and Kingsmead Comprehensive couldn't have been greater. Over the weekend someone had spray-painted swear words all over the bike shed and as I walked in, Farrow and his mates started going on at me. Mr. Simon obviously did not want to be there either, he was in a foul mood.

I was quite looking forward to catching up with Fern, though I wished I had a bit more to report about my investigations; all I had so far really was negative - that the developers probably weren't responsible for Beth's disappearance. But she, too, was in a bad mood when I caught up with her at break and didn't seem to take in what I did have to tell her.

'Something got into the kitchen garden when we were away at the weekend. It's ruined, completely ruined. Every single plant and bush has been trampled. Can't find any prints, which you'd expect if it was animals; we think it must have been people.'

'Surely no one would do that to you?'

'But it's so thoroughly destroyed. It's not eaten or chewed at, but every single thing has been wrecked. Like a giant roller's gone over it. Dad's gutted, especially, you know - that bit of the farm was so much Mum's; it's like someone's trodden all over her!' She was on the edge of tears, looking like she hadn't slept all night. I thought for a moment.

'I'd like to come back with you after school; see if there's anything I can do.'

'You can't do anything. It's hopeless.'

'Maybe. But also to see if I can get any more ideas ... anything that gives us a lead of any sort; we don't know if this has anything to do with the other business. Don't you think, we've just got to try - be open to all possibilities?'

'Spose. Okay then.'

I didn't know myself what I'd got in mind as we boarded the busy bus after school. Probably there wasn't anything I could do about the garden; but the story sounded so odd I felt it would be silly not to check out what was going on; and I also wanted to look at some of Beth's things in more detail if possible.

The bus was packed this time, being the first to leave after home-time. There were loads of people standing and we only just squeezed on and held onto the back of the driver's compartment. It was the same driver as when I'd taken Lottie out to Wheeler's Farm. Fern was squashed up nearest to him. Her mood had improved slightly since the morning. 'Hi Vince,' she said as she gave him the fare. He nodded to her, and ripped off her ticket. 'How's Patsy?' she asked.

'Same,' he replied shortly, put the bus into gear and roared off, unbalancing all the hangers-on.

'You know the driver then?' I asked as we got off at the bridge.

'Only a little. He lives not far from here at the end of the route. Mum knew his wife Patsy though, I met her a few times, she used to be quite nice. She supported Mum during the protests about the woods, right up to the end in fact. But then a funny thing happened. Vince, that guy, lost his job, he worked for the council, don't know why he lost it, and he got this driving job more or less straight away, but Patsy took it really badly. She used to be so friendly and then she seemed to have some kind of nervous breakdown when Vince was given the sack. She was off work for a few weeks and is back again, but hadn't really got better last I'd heard.'

'Where does she work?'

'At the museum in town, you know the one I mentioned.'

'No!' I told her about the woman in the shop there.

'That's her. She's completely twitchy now poor thing.'

'You can say that again.' I went on to tell her about the ribbons and the Oxfam tunic.

'That's so weird ... because that outfit did actually belong to Mum; she'd made it herself; and then one day she was in a real mood about the wood and went round the house with scissors, looking for any coloured string, any ribbons, anything she could tie on the fence; and she didn't seem to care what she cut up. She pulled out some of the ribbons, to tie on things I think. And then she lent the whole thing to Patsy who wanted to borrow it for work and said she'd repair it at the same time. Obviously she never did if it ended up like that in Oxfam. I wonder how exactly it got there. I wouldn't mind it back.'

I was thinking. 'We obviously won't get anything out of Patsy ... but I just wondered about the ladies in the Oxfam shop; they may not remember who brought it in, but it's quite unusual, maybe worth a try.'

'Yes. And it might be better if I ask,' said Fern. 'They might think it a bit odd a boy asking about women's clothing.'

'True. Will you try and find out then?'

'Straight after school tomorrow. Oh no.' We had reached the farmhouse and there was a great mess at the front door, of broken milk bottles, and spilt milk all over the steps. 'How come ...' Fern was breathing furiously.

'Could it be the geese?'

'No way. We've had milk delivered every day for as long as I can remember, and it goes in that wire crate thing by the front door, so you'd have to lift the bottles out of it first. The geese couldn't do that.'

'Is your Dad in?'

She went to the side of the house. 'No. Car's gone.'

'That's two things now, isn't it, this and the garden?'

'More like half a dozen. There've been lots of other less obvious things now I come to think of it - fences cut, greenhouse glass broken, even the henhouse. These latest are just more obviously deliberate.'

'Shouldn't you call the police? It can't go on.' She shook her head decisively. 'I'm done with them after Mum. And I think they're done with us too. They'd just say, 'Very sorry, nothing we can do, just keep an eye on things.' And go off with a little smirk on their faces.' She was striding angrily round the side of the house to show me the kitchen garden.

It really was completely destroyed. 'Whoever's done these things really has it in for your family. Can you think of anyone at all who might think they've a reason to feel that way?'

She shook her head. 'Obviously I've tried to. But I can

only come up with the police and the developers; and from what you said, they're probably not in the picture.

'Look - we can sort this lot out. Not tonight or even next month, but we can. It's not all lost, even though it'll be a lot of hard work to get it back. The lavender here, for instance, don't you cut it right back in autumn anyway? Well, it'll grow back next year if we tidy it up a bit. And some of these smaller plants: we could take cuttings and grow them in the greenhouses till they're bigger. But I think we should wait a while.'

'Cos there could be more to come?' she asked bleakly.

I nodded. 'I think now ... what we need is vigilance. Someone's waiting until you're away, or night-time, or daytime when your Dad's driven off and you're at school ... we've got to keep up a guard here and try and catch them in the act. Spot them doing these things, I don't mean confront them ourselves, but get some kind of proof of who it is. Then the police can't ignore it.'

'So I can't go to school at all. That'll please some.'

'You can't stay off all the time. Presumably your Dad's at home a fair bit. You just need to check when he will be each day. Maybe we can take it in turns for a bit to go to school. I can get off on some days. Sooner or later we're bound to spot whoever's up to these nasty tricks at the rate they're happening at the moment. And if they've stopped, well that's okay too.'

'Okay. Fine. We'll do it. Tomorrow I still want to check out Oxfam after school - I think that's urgent; and I know Dad has deliveries. Can you cover some of the afternoon?'

'Yes. Now my Dad's got this job, he's likely to walk in

with me in the morning; but the afternoon is Sport: could be handy as the boys are starting on cross-country running. Why don't you stay at home for the morning, come in around lunchtime, say you had the dentist or something and with any luck I can 'run' across for the afternoon. Just do me a little sketch map of the way you come across the fields. I think I came across the start of the track at the weekend.

'I'll show you it now.'

We walked through the greenhouses and the small, overgrown fields to a slope which rose gradually to meet an edge of the woods. We climbed up a worn field path of chalk and flints and soon reached the boundary of the wood. Here we met a broader track that ran round next to the trees. We turned left onto this and it circled around the shoulder of the hill then dipped into the woods, crossing another small track. 'That's the way up to the den, by the way,' said Fern. I recognised this bit from the weekend. But we didn't go up, just continued on a level until the track left the trees and came out in the large, stubble-covered field I'd come past from school the day I bunked off.

'Okay, so I'll come back this way around midday, when you'll go in to school, and then do Oxfam after. I'll wait out here until you get back, in case your Dad's not in. If he is in I won't let him see me.'

'Fine.'

∾

It was teatime by the time I got home that evening, everyone else was at home.

'Where've you been?' Dad asked.

'Out at Wheeler's Farm with Fern.'

'You should let us know if you're going to be late.'

'Okay. But you've not been bothered about where I've been up to now.' I answered back defiantly. I was tired and some of Fern's anger seemed to have rubbed off on me.

'No need for cheek. Just tell us where you're going and when you'll be back.' The trouble was now Dad was better and back to his old self he was much firmer and more likely to keep an eye on things and put his foot down.

'Good day at the office?' I changed the subject, slightly tongue in cheek.

'No, actually. It's a shambles. But I'll sort it out soon. What about school?'

'Complete crap, actually.'

'Louis!' said Mum who had come into the room.

'Well it was. You two think you're the only ones with hard days sometimes.' I marched off to do my homework.

13 Vigilance and Sore Feet

I was careful to remember my running gear the next morning before I set off with Dad. 'We're doing cross-country this afternoon. I'll probably be late home,' I said, making it sound like the two statements were connected, although if anything cross-country was more likely to get you home early as it started early.

This was handy, as I'd thought it would be, as I set off straight after lunch. But I'd forgotten that I wouldn't be alone. We were sent on a route over the field, the way I wanted to go initially; but then the path turned right towards town and I wanted to go left to the woods. The other boys were a bit of a nuisance. Quite a few dropped off the moment we were out of sight of the school, and sloped off home. I found myself jogging next to Mervyn, who said, 'How's your witchy friend then?' I ignored this and swung off to the left, as he bleated on about me going the wrong way.

As always it was a relief to enter the woods after being at school. The coolness and the quiet calmed you down. I felt like dawdling in the trees, but had promised to get to the farm as soon as I could. As I came out of the wood at the top of the field and looked down at the farm, something caught my eye. It was Mr Woodruff's car door opening and reflecting the sun. He loaded some boxes in the back and switched on the engine. I kept still against the trees. Then the front door of the farm opened and Fern came out, carrying her schoolbag. So he was taking her in by car on his way somewhere. She would just be in time for afternoon school. I settled in for what would probably be a long wait.

But I'd come prepared. I'd slipped the paperback that Fern had lent me into the baggy pocket of my shorts, so I got this out determined to read it at last. There was a comfortable tree trunk to lean against, so I made a start, glancing up every few seconds at the farmhouse. I decided it was best to watch things from here, because if anyone else was watching the farmhouse for an opportunity, I didn't want them to see me arrive there. Also, from here I had a really good view: I could cover the whole of the house and outbuildings, including the farm workers' cottages, greenhouses, kitchen garden, and also parts of the lane where it left the farm by the duck pond and a stretch where it joined the main road. The only bit of the lane I couldn't see was hidden by the cluster of trees that blocked the farm from sight from the main road. But I could see the beginning and end of the lane, so that should cover it. It was a nice, warm sunny spot and it was a relief after rushing around so much to sit there and relax for a few hours. I would just have to make sure I didn't doze off.

I spent a long time reading though it passed quickly. In the tree book I found a section on tree spirits. It was a bit surprising to read about an East European one called Leshy, a spirit of the forest. What got me was that he was supposed to wear his clothes back to front. I thought back to the weird time at the weekend when wearing my jacket back to front seemed to allow me to hear Duir the oak tree; this Leshy apparently varied enormously in height, from dwarf to giant size, and disappeared for parts of the year. He usually came out around October, about now, and kept going till Spring, when he could become quite dangerous (it didn't mention how). He was generally good-natured, but naughty and liked leading people astray in the forest, though always releasing his victims in the end. He had no shadow and made all kinds of noises: whistling, shouting, sobbing and moaning, calling out like a bird of prey, and sometimes laughing like mad women.

I remembered the day I'd first discovered the giant oak Duir and the strange noises I'd heard before the storm and the sense of being led round and round in circles in a panic. It sounded just like the sort of thing this creature would get up to, if you could believe in him. But the panic and getting lost could happen to anyone at any time. Just then something caught my eye on the main road. A car was turning into the lane. It wasn't Mr. Woodruff's. It carried on, like a small beetle from this distance, then I lost it as the lane passed next to the island of woodland. I waited for it to reappear. I waited; and waited some more. Nothing. This was really odd; I'd had my eyes glued to the lane where it came out near the farmhouse, until they watered. I didn't even blink. But once anything emerged near the house it was unlikely to be hidden from view unless it went round the side towards the kitchen garden. I sat and waited some more, sure that soon something would happen, even if it turned back to the main road. I must have sat like that for a few hours.

It started to get colder. The sun had gone. I wondered what had happened to Fern and Mr. Woodruff. Also I realised that if I didn't leave now, I'd miss the last bus from the end of the lane and have to walk home through the woods which would soon be dark; and I'd be extremely late.

I got up, chilly now with sitting still in sweaty sports gear for so long, and started jogging down the flint and chalk path to the farm. I glanced briefly at the house and outbuildings which looked shut-up and abandoned; all the ducks, geese and hens had gone to sleep. I felt like saying goodnight to Chanticleer, but couldn't risk waking them all up; besides, I had to hurry.

I left the farmyard on the dirt-track that turned into the tarmac lane near the main road. As I drew close to the patch of woodland I stared hard into the darkness of the trees, but could see nothing. It really was getting dark now. I hadn't realised, it was happening much earlier now we were getting into autumn. It was a bit spooky, so I hurried on along the track which had grass down the middle and two deep wheel ruts either side. I tripped on a clump of grass that I didn't see in the deep dusk, so moved over to one of the ruts which was worn smooth. I was just nearing the end of the stretch beside the wood and nearly up to the easier tarmac part when I felt a sharp pain in the sole of my foot. I stopped and pulled off my trainer. A patch of blood spread rapidly over my sock from the sole of my foot. I looked at the underside of the trainer. There was a huge steel tack with a very sharp point and a flat head embedded in it. I looked at the ground where I'd stepped. I could just make out about half a dozen more tacks in the rut, all resting upside down on their flat bases. They could not have been dropped accidently as most would have landed on their sides. These had been put there deliberately like this; they were, in fact, spaced evenly apart. And in the wheel rut where a car couldn't avoid them. This had to be the same person who had done all the other things at the farm. I picked them up carefully and put them in my pocket. I felt scared now: the tacks could not have been there when Mr. Woodruff left or he would have got no further than the main road with a flat tyre; someone had been here while I had been keeping watch. Not very successfully it seemed. And I hadn't seen them leave. That left only the patch of woodland for them to be hiding in. My heart was beating very fast now; I couldn't see anything against the dark woods in this light, but if they were looking out, waiting, watching, they could see me. I tried to look straight ahead, but kept glancing to the right out of the corner of my eye. Now I just wanted to catch that bus and get home. I would tell Mum and Dad all about it now; they'd be bound to see that something had to be done. My foot hurt with every step where the tack had spiked it and was bleeding quite a bit into the trainer. It felt yucky and squelchy. My breath came in short gasps as I hurried to catch the bus. I desperately wanted to get past the trees, they seemed black and menacing now. I kept thinking I could hear sounds coming from them; perhaps just animals; but I couldn't convince myself. Suddenly a huge black shape roared out of the woods in front of me - a car. I shook with fright. But it turned up the lane to the main road. It had no lights on, until it reached the road and they were switched on. I had just made out that it was a dark-coloured estate car of some sort. It turned right at the end of the lane, away from town, and as I watched it roar off into the distance, I saw a taller set of lights coming along the road - my bus. I started to run and got there just as it drew up.

'You look all in,' said the friendly woman driving the bus.

'Got lost doing cross country' I muttered as I handed over the fare.

'Your Mum'll be wondering where you are.'

∞

She was. So was Dad. He was outside Oaklands looking up and down the estate. 'Where the hell have you been?' he demanded.

Mum came out hearing his voice. 'You're really late. Has something happened?'

'I got a bit lost in cross country. Then I ended up at Wheeler's Farm...'

'Lost my foot!' Dad exploded. 'We've been up and down this road for the last hour. Met one of your classmates who said he'd finished cross country hours ago, but that you'd bunked off halfway to go to the woods!'

Thanks Mervyn. 'Well that's true. But I also had something I needed to do ... there have been a lot of funny things going on at Wheeler's Farm recently -'

'I'm not interested in what's going on at Wheeler's Farm. What did I say to you only last night?'

'We've been really worried,' added Mum.

'I'm sorry. But you didn't worry about me at all before - so I'm not used to needing to let you know where I'm going all the time.'

'Well you can get used to it. And you can come home with me for the rest of this week and stay at home.'

'But you don't come home till five.'

'You can get the bus into town, wait in the Parks Office in the Council for me. You obviously can't be trusted at the moment. I'm not having you running around the countryside at all hours, getting involved with who knows what.'

Little did he know. So I was grounded. Just when I needed to be out and about investigating. And no chance of even going to the woods just to get away from it all. It was so unfair. There was no way I was going to turn to them for help now. Just when I was starting to think it was maybe all too big for me, I was on my own.

14 An Alphabet of Trees

But there was still Fern. I told her all that had happened the next day. She was amazed and angry when I told her about the tacks and the car. "Whoever it is is so spiteful and sneaky!'

She had also been busy. 'I got the tunic back. And the woman in Oxfam did remember who'd brought it in - they'd thought it a bit odd because it was a man. Someone middle-aged they'd seen about the town they said, who parked his estate car right on the pavement outside the shop. Sounded just like Patsy's husband - you remember, the bus driver, Vince?'

'Yes. Estate car?'

'Yes.'

'That was what I saw last night!'

'What, you think he could be the person who's done all those things at our place?'

'It's possible. Unless someone else was driving his car, or, as is quite likely, there are other people in the area with estate cars. It's so frustrating I'm grounded.'

'Yes. I'm sorry you got into all that trouble. And thanks for sitting it out yesterday, it was worth it. Dad was okay about me having the morning off, I said I was exhausted -

which was true in a way. But I didn't spot anything. But now you've found out all this, I might do a bit of snooping myself ... around Vince's place if I can pick a time he and Patsy are both at work; straight after school should be okay if he's working today. I wasn't worried about keeping an eye on the farm today as Dad's at home, making up orders. I'm not telling him about all this just yet, he's just so worried about everything he wouldn't cope with me doing these things.'

'No. I made that mistake with mine. Thinking he'd realise what was most important - me being a bit late home, or catching criminals. But be careful, won't you?'

'You sound just like Dad!'

∿

At the end of the day there were two buses waiting to go in opposite directions outside school. Fern got on the one going to the villages, I took the town bus. The driver was Vince. I avoided looking at him as I put down the exact fare and moved along quickly. I wasn't sure if he could have seen me last night, if it had been him. But he completely ignored me. As I sat down by the window I saw Fern waving at me from the window of the other bus. She tilted her head slightly in Vince's direction and gave me a brief thumbs-up, which I took to mean, the coast was clear as far as he was concerned.

I got off at the town centre and walked through the shopping centre where we'd spent our brief happy family spell at the weekend. I found the Council offices easily and Parks was round the back where a number of council maintenance trucks were kept. Normally I would have been quite interested to visit Dad's work. Today, though, I could feel my face developing a sulky expression as I approached, just because of why I was here. My foot still hurt, I wondered if it had got infected because I'd been sent straight to bed without a bath, and had been too proud to tell them about it.

I slouched into a large room with sheets of work rotas on the walls and an old bloke locking away some equipment. 'Now what's the betting you're the new boss's lad!' he said in a friendly way. I nodded neutrally. 'You might have a bit of a wait; we was a bit behind with things here today. That's your Dad's office in there'. He nodded at an empty room with a counter and a computer on a desk. 'You can sit in there if you like. I'm off home soon.'

There was nothing at all to do in the main room, so I went and inspected Dad's office. It was both bare and messy, with nothing but the desk, a filing cabinet and a pile of used internal mail envelopes. I sat in the only chair and twizzled for a bit in it, feeling bored, and frustrated that I wasn't out roaming the woods or looking for things at the farm. Then one of the envelopes caught my eye. There were lots of boxes with names on the front, crossed out to reuse and send to the next person. But the last name on most of the envelopes was Vince Price. Could this be the Vince who had just driven me into town? I remembered Fern had said he used to work for the Council until he got the sack. So had he done Dad's job? I searched through the envelopes quickly, looking for any other clues. I soon came upon one: a typed envelope from outside with the whole of the Council's address on it and his position, Parks Manager. Dad's job. A cupboard door slamming in the room next to me reminded me of the old guy. I wondered if he could tell me anything that would help me identify this Vince. I sauntered out and found him putting his jacket on. 'Did you know the boss before my Dad?'

'Did I ever. Miserable old sod. We was all glad to see the back of him. Your Dad's a right breath of fresh air.'

Not always my experience. 'Do you know where he went when he left?'

'Bus driver I heard.'

'Do you know why he left?'

'Got the sack. Some equipment went missing; it was an odd business. But we wasn't sorry to see him go. Now I must go or I'll be in hot water with the Missus.'

We said goodbye and I went and sat down again to think properly. There was no doubt in my mind, now, that Vince the bus driver was the same Vince that had done Dad's job before him, and was not a very nice person. In other words, perhaps capable of the things that had happened at the farm. And Beth's disappearance? Then I looked at the computer. I quickly glanced out of the door. Nobody was out there now and no sign of Dad yet. I joggled the mouse.

The screen crackled into life with a message, 'Please enter your password.' Damn, I thought. I tried 'Vince' and 'Patsy,' but with no luck. I was stuck without a password. Then I heard footsteps. Dad. I quickly shut down the screen and resumed my twizzling on the chair. 'Hello there,' said Dad.

'Hi.'

'Okay?'

'Mm. Do you use this computer much?'

'I haven't had time to get an account set up yet, but it

should happen in the next day or two.'

So soon Vince's documents would be removed from the system. And there was no way I could get into them unless I had his password.

The bus back from town was crowded and we didn't talk at all. When we reached the estate it was still light and I looked longingly up at the woods, but knew it was no good arguing with Dad. Mum and Lottie were not coming back for another hour, and I decided to go on the computer for a bit. I thought I would look up those strange symbols from Beth's study that Fern had called 'Ogham,' see if there was anything about it on the internet.

There was quite a bit. It was pronounced 'Oh-am,' it said. One website called it the 'Beth, Louis, Fern alphabet,' How strange, our three names! They formed the first three letters of a twenty-letter alphabet. And each of the symbols stood for a particular tree. Beth had the symbol T which stood for birch; Louis had the symbol TT, which stood for rowan - also my middle name. And Fern, TTT, stood for alder. All these trees and those that followed had special features. Birch had many medicinal uses and was associated with new beginnings; it said that birch trees were often the first to grow in treeless areas of land; but they were also associated with self-sacrifice, since they tended to get overshadowed and die off as larger trees moved in and their remains enriched the soil. I thought about Beth the person. From what I had pieced together she had certainly made personal sacrifices by camping out in the woods to try and save them. I hoped that was as far as her sacrifice went.

Louis, the rowan had many associations; the one I already knew, 'birdcatcher'; also, 'friend or protector of cattle.' I thought of the Jersey cows back at our farm; I hadn't done much to protect them. The rowan was also known as the 'Quickbeam', or 'tree of life', and 'delight of the eye.' I didn't think anyone except maybe Mum would think me a delight to the eye. But apparently the rowan also scored highly on knowledge and special powers; it was associated with magic and its wood was used for wands. Then there was the bit about 'wattles of knowledge'; it said they used to make a sort of platform of rowan twigs as a bed for a person to lie on and go into a trance which would allow him to gain access to all sorts of hidden knowledge. I thought of the trees in the wood and all their understanding of things that had happened and were going to happen. I wondered if I had gone into a sort of trance when I had heard them singing and talking. If I could deliberately put myself in this state, maybe I'd learn more.

I looked up rowan on another website. Some of the sites were pretty weird and into magic and witchcraft; I wasn't very keen on all that, but thought some of the ancient meanings given to trees were interesting. This other site said that the expression, 'On the wattles of knowledge' came from rowan wattles and meant doing one's utmost to get information. Well that fitted with what I was trying to do now, even if not very successfully.

There was quite a bit about Fern, the alder. The trees had a number of practical uses; three kinds of dye could be extracted from it, and it had very water-resistant wood so was good for building things that needed to stand in water like jetties. It was also described as a 'guardian of the milk,' which was maybe because milk buckets were thought to have been made from it. Shields used to be made from alder wood and the tree was also called 'shield of the heart;' did this mean Fern would be good at looking after things to do with feelings? Cutting down the alder was said to lead to the burning down of a person's house, or to it getting struck by lightning. It also said rowan twigs could protect against lightning strikes.

There were similar descriptions of a number of other trees. It was fascinating and the coincidence with our names was very odd indeed. But apart from telling me a little more about Beth's interests, it did not seem to get me any further in my search for her. I wondered if Fern had found anything out up at Vince's house.

∾

In the morning I met her outside school after a rather silent walk through the estate with Dad who caught his bus at the shops. She came down the field path from the woods. 'Didn't feel like being on the same bus as Vince, somehow, and the woods were lovely - all bright and fresh and autumn colours. Made me want to stay there.'

'I'll bet,' I said enviously. 'Any luck yesterday?'

'Nothing much on Vince, well not directly. Oh, except, he does have an estate car. It was there outside Vine cottage. But I bungled it all a bit, as I was so confident he wouldn't be back I hung around a bit, forgetting Patsy might be. And she came up the street just as I'd slipped into the front garden to look for any clues, which was very awkward. So I had to pretend

I'd been coming to visit her. But that was quite interesting in itself; she seemed very touched that I should visit her and made me welcome with tea and biscuits and all that; and I learnt something really odd.'

'What was that?'

'That she did give the tunic back to Mum, and, she did repair it just before that. She said she'd bought some ribbons in town, but they were very slightly wider than the original ones, and she wasn't sure if they were okay for mum; so she just threaded them through where the old ones had been, without sewing the ends down, so they could easily be pulled out if Mum wasn't happy with it. Only she apparently had been more than happy and put it on and kept it on even though it was a very hot day. And that was the last time Patsy saw her.'

'Which was when?'

'Last day of July. The day she disappeared. Patsy had gone up to visit her in the wood early in the morning with some breakfast and the mended tunic and Mum asked her if she could stay, but she said she had to get back for work as they were getting difficult about all her time off. She was really upset telling me all this, she started crying a bit. She said if only she'd stayed with her, maybe she'd still be with us.' Fern herself sounded pretty upset now, but was in control. 'Anyway, then she told me Mum hadn't wanted to take the skirt as she was wearing jeans and said she'd get that another time. And now, Patsy said, she wears it herself a lot as it comforts her and reminds her of Mum. I didn't get a chance to tell her about rescuing it from Oxfam, because another odd thing happened; although she'd been so welcoming, she suddenly looked at the clock and saw the time and said I should go because my Dad would be wondering where I was. I said it was fine, and she said, Vince would be home soon and she needed to get his dinner ready. So I went. But she said to come again any time after school but make it early.

'Well! What do you make of all that?' I asked.

'Well Vince must have taken the tunic in - it sounds like him and his car - so he must have been the last person to have seen Mum. And Patsy isn't involved - she misses Mum, that's obvious; and she's a bit scared of Vince.'

We looked at each other. I didn't like the sound of it, but wasn't going to say so; though probably it didn't need saying. Instead, I told her about what I'd heard at the Council. 'If only I could get into his account. That password. What other names do people use as passwords? Their kids?'

'Doesn't have any. His car had the letters VIN on the number plate though. Maybe try that if you get a chance.'

∽

I did, after hurrying from school into town to give me time at Dad's computer before he came for me. But it wasn't the right word. I was aware of the time; any minute now Dad could walk in and catch me. The old guy who'd been there yesterday was banging about and kept interrupting me with cheerful little jokes. I didn't want to ask him any more about Vince or it would look funny. Time was ticking by; Dad would be here any moment; and probably his account would have replaced Vince's in a day or two. I chewed at my fingernails, raking over every bit of information I had on him. Okay, so

Vince was someone who liked putting his name on things as he'd got that number plate on his car. What was it he'd called his house? something cottage ... Vine Cottage. Presumably after himself too. I typed in 'Vine' without much hope. And Bingo! In front of me was Vince's desktop. I opened up the emails. My heart pounding, I scanned through work messages from other departments, and one from his boss summoning him for a meeting; interesting, but nothing particularly useful for our purposes. Then I checked his documents. And there I found it. The letter supposed to be from Beth to Mr. Woodruff about why she'd left him. I was shaking with excitement now. I looked around to see if the printer was switched on and heard footsteps - Dad's. Quickly I closed it all down and jumped up, saying 'hello' very enthusiastically to cover my agitation. He seemed surprised, but relieved to find me apparently more friendly. We left the building together and as we sat down on the bus, he said, 'Phew, Friday tomorrow! Glad the weekend's in sight. I should think you could go home on your own tomorrow if you want. You've shown me I can rely on you enough now.'

No. I needed to come back and print that letter. 'Oh I don't mind. I quite like coming in and seeing where you work. And maybe you could show me round a bit more.'

Dad seemed surprised and gratified by this interest. 'Well, okay, I'll see if I can finish a bit earlier.' Oh no, that wouldn't do. I needed time alone in his office.

'What sort of time can you get off?' I asked reluctantly.

'Maybe an hour earlier. If I work through lunch.'

'Well don't miss your lunch just because of me.'

'No, no it's fine,' he insisted.

I couldn't sleep that night and wished Fern's phone hadn't been cut off recently as I couldn't wait till the next day to tell her. But I had to.

15 The Trail of the Trees

I caught up with Fern at break and told her all.

'Great work!' she breathed. She'd gone quite pink with excitement.

'I just hope I can get there before Dad.'

'Could you leave at afternoon break maybe?'

'Good thinking. Will do.'

So I sneaked out at three and waited for the bus. But nothing came for half an hour - it wasn't the busy time. I was scared someone would see me from the classrooms. But finally one pulled up, empty. It was the woman driver from the other night. She didn't recognise me.

When I walked into the Parks Department there were many more council workers around, slamming metal lockers and generally winding up for the day. A few stared, but I ignored them. The old guy had not knocked off yet. Luckily, Dad's office was empty, so I marched in looking confident and switched on the computer. It said, 'Welcome to Windows Tom Stuart.' My heart sank. A day too late. Did that mean all Vince's documents had been lost? Surely some people would be able to recover these things. The police, for instance.

Just then, Dad walked in. He stopped in surprise seeing me there. 'You're very early aren't you? It's only quarter to four.'

'I wasn't feeling too well. And ... I was just looking to see if you had any games on this thing,' I added lamely, not sure if that was convincing illness behaviour.

Dad was silent. Then said, 'Well we'd better get you home then. Skip the tour.'

What a stuff-up. Now I'd have to stay in all evening; I'd hoped to get in a bit of time in the woods.

At home, I lay on my bunk, suddenly really tired from the tension of the last few days, and not sleeping last night. And feeling defeated for now, with losing the email before I'd printed the evidence. Surely now it was time we went to the police - the evidence must be retrievable if only they would agree to look for it.

∾

But Fern, who I met up at the den on Saturday, as we' d agreed the day before, thought not. 'They'll just dismiss us as two silly kids. You don't know what they're like. They're really blinkered and complacent and also pretty lazy. We've got to do this ourselves still, until we've got evidence we can wave in their faces, go to the paper with, or whatever.'

I had another idea. 'Do you remember those ribbons I told you about on the fence?'

'Mmm. I've seen them too.'

'Well, if Patsy said the ones she'd added were a bit larger, we could compare those on the fence with those on the tunic, and at least find out if they were put there before or after Beth disappeared.'

'Good idea. I've got the tunic right here.' She rather shyly pulled out from a box a whole collection of things to do with Beth - her photo, some letters and a scarf, and the tunic she had bought back from Oxfam.

We climbed down quickly, not forgetting to close up the tree at the bottom, and made our way down the hillside, to the path I'd come up last Saturday after meeting the developer's delivery men. There was no one around today and we could see the ribbons on the fence fluttering in the breeze.

Fern put the tunic up against the fence and we compared the ribbons. The ones on the fence were about five millimetres wider. 'So. These came out of the tunic the day she disappeared. Why would she tie some more on, just then?' I wondered.

'As ... as a signal?' Fern suggested. 'Look - this white one is wound about the fence in a particular way, not just tied - it's in a T-shape.'

'Or Beth shape - it could be an Ogham symbol,' I said suddenly, remembering what I'd read on the internet.

'Yes, a sort of 'Beth was here,' do you think?' Fern grew excited.

'Mmm. But we pretty much knew that anyway. But I wonder what else it could mean. Could it be, for example, the first of a few markers like that?' I was thinking of how we'd found Lottie that time, by following her accidental trail through the wood.

'Perhaps. We should look around for more things nearby, shouldn't we? But I feel like I've done that so many times already since she disappeared, especially round here.'

We decided to try again anyway, and combed the area as systematically as we could, working over metre by metre, until we found ourselves at the edge of the road. There was nothing. Tired and hungry, we agreed to meet back at the tree after lunch to work on the whole thing again.

∾

I arrived at the den first, and lay back in the afternoon sun and relaxed while I waited, gazing up into the half-bare autumn branches. As I looked into the criss-crossing twigs they seemed to shape themselves into patterns; some looked just like parts of the Ogham alphabet. Perhaps it was similar to when you're little: all cars seem to have faces at the front, with two headlight eyes and the radiator grill for a mouth. All branches have twigs coming off them and the Ogham alphabet could easily be made of twigs. What could Beth have been trying to tell us with that ribbon? Then I remembered last time I'd been up here on my own, and my strange conversation with Duir; and my idea of putting myself into a trance. Also, I could put my clothes on backwards. I'd left my jacket behind after lunch as it was so warm; but I had a sweatshirt I could turn around. I did this, and lay back and waited.

Nothing seemed to happen at first. I closed my eyes and tried to empty my mind of all the thoughts that had been whizzing round it. It wasn't easy. But gradually, as I relaxed more deeply, I began to sense that vibration I'd felt before. Then a very faint booming sound, a bit like some morse code message. Finally, the sounds started to take shape; 'Follow the signs ... be broad in beam and mind ... the way is through the trees ... the trees that are you ...'

'Duir?' I whispered.

'I am here. But I am old and evil influences are drawing my strength ... my strength is going. I cannot say ... much more.'

'Please stay!' I almost shouted, suddenly afraid of losing him.

'I will protect you ... while you are in need. And then you must care for my descendants. Now I must rest.'

'Goodbye.' I said anxiously. Then there was quiet. I just rested, waiting, feeling a bit oddly upset.

Then there was a rustling at the bottom of the tree and Fern arrived. 'Why are you wearing your top back to front?' I told her what I had just heard.

'Follow the signs ... the trees that are you ... what trees are we?'

'We are Beth, Louis, Fern,' I suddenly realised. 'The birch, the rowan and the alder.'

'Of course. I'd forgotten about those,' she said. 'I think it means ... we must look for those trees ... and signs in those trees perhaps?'

I wasn't sure. 'We could try. So shall we start with birch? Where would we find them?'

'Back down near the road. Between the bus stop by the wood and the stretch leading to towards the river.' She led the way. We went past the ribbons again, through the developer's patch and onto a very narrow track I'd not seen before. In a little while we came to the birch grove. It was open and sunny, with a thin carpet of little yellow birch leaves. The delicate black fingers of the branches hung down against the shiny white bark. We looked around for signs. I checked all the tree trunks carefully. 'But she wouldn't carve anything on a tree' Fern reminded me. We felt a bit stuck after a while and sat down on a big rock in the sun.

'Maybe we're barking up the wrong tree, ha, ha.' I was swinging my leg - it always helps me to think, and swept aside some of the carpet of leaves with my foot, leaving bare soil. And there it was, a sign as clear as anything. A 'T' symbol, scraped deep in the soil with a stick or something. Obviously made before the autumn leaves started falling. We stared in amazement. I don't think either of us had really expected to find anything so clear.

But now we realised we were onto something, we worked frantically at clearing the other leaves away. Fern found us two small fallen birch branches to use as brooms, and we swept the leaves lightly so we wouldn't rub out any faint markings. Again, at first there was nothing; and then Fern called out. 'Over here!' It was another 'T'. 'It's by the path, I think that must mean to follow the path, do you?'

'Yes, let's.' As we walked, I considered what we were looking for next. 'So we've found 'birch'; that leaves rowan and alder ... I know where some rowan trees are, right next to the estate. But it's a long way from here, and in the opposite direction to the one we've so far been guided towards.'

'Yes, it is. Maybe there are others. But I know where the alders are. By the river.'

'Well that's not far now. Shall we check them out first?'

'Okay.'

It was still a little way. We were hugging the very edge of the wood on the little track, but still in the trees, kind of parallel with the road but a long way from it. In the distance I could see the white bridge where the bus stop for the farm was. Eventually we reached the river where it emerged from the trees. I could see the alder trees a few hundred yards ahead upstream. Fern stopped suddenly. Her face looked strained.

'What's the matter?'

'I don't know. I don't feel well. It's my stomach. Probably a bit of indigestion after rushing up here after lunch.'

'Why don't you sit down for a bit by the water?'

'No I want to do this -' she grimaced suddenly.

'Okay, look, I'll go on slowly, checking thoroughly, and if I find anything I'll call, or come back for you. If you rest for a few minutes now it might go away and you can join me.' She agreed reluctantly and sat down on a grassy bank hugging her knees.

I plodded on slowly, searching the path by the river. It was really warm for the time of year and it would have been nice to rest by the water, even paddle. But there was not time for that sort of thing now that we were onto something. I rounded a bend in the river and could no longer see Fern. Then stopped. There was a man bending over at the base of one of the alder trunks at the edge of the water. When he straightened up I saw he had an axe. I was about to turn round and run for it when I saw ropes and realised he was about to chop down some small alder trees; and that he was the skip man who had gone on about Chanticleer. Not someone I took to, but probably not dangerous. He scowled when he saw me and said, 'What you doing out here then?'

'I was going to ask you that. Are you thinking of cutting down those trees?'

'Not thinking. Going to. Alder wood. Very good for kitchens and bathrooms. And it's all free!'

'Well hang on a minute. This isn't your land is it?'

'Ah no, but I got permission from the guy who does own it to take away as much as I can carry,' he said with an unpleasant triumphant leer, and without another word struck his first blow with the axe. I felt like telling him it would be a long time before it was usable for his kitchen, but it didn't seem a good idea to argue with someone like that, or indeed much point.

I couldn't do what I wanted with him around so I turned back to find Fern. Just as I rounded the bend and caught sight of her, I heard a kind of shriek from behind me - like a human voice but not quite. Fern looked up, jumped up and ran towards me. I looked back. The skip man was running towards us, his face bright red and sweating, still grasping the axe. His hands were covered in red stuff - my first thought was that he had chopped off a hand or finger. But he waved them, uninjured, at me, shouting something about the 'bleeding screaming trees.' Fern had reached us by now, white as a sheet, and stared as he charged madly on. 'Do you need help?' she called.

'No but get out of there!' he yelled. We stared at each other in amazement.

'Come on, let's go and see,' said Fern, pale but fearless.

We rounded the bend once more and a small chopped alder lay half-in, half-out of the river. there was red stuff all over the exposed cut end that stuck out of the water. 'Did he cut himself?' I wondered.

'No it's just alder sap. It's red,' Fern informed me. 'He obviously thought it was blood too.'

'And the scream, did you hear that?'

'Yes, I thought it was you, so I came.'

'No, it wasn't ... it seemed to happen just as the tree was cut down.' We stared at each other.

'What a waste of a tree.' said Fern eventually. We stood and looked at the mess. He had left all his ropes and things behind. 'It really freaked him, didn't it?' I said with satisfaction, thinking how smug he'd been a few minutes earlier.

'And so it should. It's very unlucky to cut down alders!' She sat down next to it.

'How's your stomach?'

'Not good. Worse, really. Maybe all this is getting to me.' She leant forward grasping her knees. And then gasped and pointed. 'Look!' Tangled in the fallen alder branches just above where its top branches dipped into the water was a single blue ribbon. It was very frayed, dirty and only just recognisable as one of Beth's. It was tied round something. I got hold of the cut end of the tree that rested on the bank and pulled it back onto the grass. Fern supported the lighter end nearer the water as it came up and she reached for the ribbon. It was tied onto something. A little stick. She disentangled it hurriedly. 'This is one of Mum's Ogham sticks! Look, it's alder.' The stick had the triple downstrokes for the symbol

Fern scraped onto it. 'It's hers!' murmured Fern. 'She came here ... oh where is she now?' I noticed she was shivering violently.

We talked a bit about where we could go from here. Rowan was the next obvious thing to try; but the only rowans we knew of were a distance from here back at the estate. I said, 'We're getting somewhere at last I think. But we'd better call it a day - it's getting late and you're not well.

'I want to carry on, we can't stop now.'

'We have to think ahead. It's nearly dark. If I'm out late again, I'll be grounded again and that'll be a disaster. She saw the sense of this and agreed to wait till tomorrow when we could start again. We agreed to meet at the den in Duir. I walked with her along the riverbank to the white bridge. She turned off into her lane. Then just as we'd said goodbye she called back.

'Louis. There's just one other thing that might not take long. I kept remembering it and then forgetting again. This little wood.' We were very close to the place where the car had disappeared and I'd found the tacks. Getting caught up with all the other stuff I'd forgotten it too. We decided to have a quick look. We found the tyre marks and followed them into the trees. It wasn't quite as late as the other night but still felt gloomy and spooky. I was secretly glad there were two of us this time. It was a really dense little patch of woodland. A sudden crackle of twigs made us both jump and silently we reached for each other's hands. The tyre marks came to an end and the trees seemed to close around us. Then I notice a small track to the right, going yet deeper into the woods. It was hard going through very dense undergrowth. After only a few metres it stopped, and we found ourselves in front of a battered old shed with a heavy padlock on the door. There was no way of getting that open. But there was a window, covered in cobwebs on the inside. I could feel Fern's hand trembling now. I put my fingers round the window frame and pulled. The frame came away, it was rotten and I put the whole thing on the ground, leaving a gaping hole. We collided as we both tried to look in at once.

It was black, you couldn't see a thing. 'I think I'd better go first.' I said firmly, not liking to think what I might find. With some difficulty and lots of scrapes and cuts, I squeezed through the small opening. I waited a few moments for my eyes to adjust, then called out 'Hello?' There was no answer. I looked around. In the gloom I made out some large square objects ... cardboard boxes. Nervously I felt inside one. Something cold and hard; a can of something. I took it to the window space framed by Fern's anxious face. 'See if you can read this.' I handed it out.

'It says ... Baked Beans.' I went back and checked the rest. It was all food stores, like tinned spaghetti. I climbed out. We trudged back through the trees, no longer on edge, but quietly disappointed. And yet, it could have been worse.

16 Chanticleer's Flight

At home, Mum and Dad were busy talking about some problem at Mum's work. I played cards with Lottie until it was time for her bed. I went early myself so I could have a good long read of the book I'd borrowed. Although we seemed to have been getting somewhere, I wasn't sure what we were going to do next. I needed inspiration.

I opened the book at random. I found myself looking at a picture of a giant ash tree called Yggdrasil. It was supposed to stretch round the whole world, with its roots deep in the underworld. One root led to a fountain which fed it; another was the source of wisdom. A nasty-looking serpent was nibbling away at the roots. On the highest branches of the tree there was a golden cockerel, and deer came and fed off the branches. As well as being a tree, it was a horse belonging to the Norse god Odin. Apparently it was always under threat from evil demons who kept on trying to destroy it.

A pretty busy tree, this Yggdrasil. In the Ogham alphabet the ash was called Nion and had the symbol ⟙⟙⟙. Like the other trees it meant a number of different things. It was called 'Checker of the peace': its wood was used for spears.

Another meaning it had was 'flight of women' and 'flight of beauty'. This was a bit harder to understand but seemed to be to do with magicians coming across obstacles in their work and being helped by a beautiful and clever goddess; apparently this could apply to people who just felt a bit stuck. That was me, I thought; rowan, 'my' tree, was meant to represent magical powers. Certainly I'd benefitted from inspiration in the trees, and couldn't get any further in our search at the moment. Maybe I needed to find an ash tree. I didn't think I'd seen any in the wood. Perhaps we should now be looking around the group of rowans near the estate. Or should we just go back to that hut full of tinned food? I must have fallen asleep because next day I was not at all sure what to do.

I decided to check out the rowan trees and go and talk to Fern up at the den. When I got to the stairs I passed the skip man leaning out of his window smoking. When he saw me, he slammed the window shut and disappeared. This was a bit odd. But he'd been behaving oddly yesterday too - the alder tree had obviously freaked him out. His kitchen didn't seem to be getting anywhere. I noticed lots of takeaway boxes outside, overflowing from his rubbish bin. Presumably he couldn't cook while he had no kitchen. Then I remembered the shed full of tins. Could there be a connection there? Maybe it was his car that came and went into the little wood to get himself a meal. Why hide them away though? Maybe they had been stolen or something. Tins were easy enough to deal with without a kitchen, just a camping stove, or maybe he had a campfire somewhere in the wood. In which case, could he be the person behind the nasty events at the farm?

He didn't seem like a very nice person, chopping down those trees. We hadn't been very vigilant lately, we'd have to keep watch a bit more.

I scrambled up to the rowan trees. They were a brilliant sight at the moment, with their ripe, red berries: a real 'delight to the eye.' There were only about half a dozen of them, and as I approached lots of small birds flew up from the branches where they'd been having a feast on the berries. The leaves were bright orange, but hadn't yet fallen, so the scrubby grass and earth underneath was easy to see. I searched methodically for signs of any sort, hoping and hoping to come across something like yesterday. But after almost an hour, I could find nothing, My head bumped against a large ripe bunch of berries about to fall, and I decided to pick it in case Chanticleer fancied some; it felt like a long time since I'd seen him and our searches were bound to go somewhere near the farm. I made my way into the woods to meet up with Fern at the den.

As I approached the summit where Duir stood, firm and tall, I remembered the words, 'look after my descendants.' Well, his descendants were all about my feet, I realised, in the shape of acorns. I filled my pockets with handfuls of them to take home later. Then, as I was about to make the final climb, there was a rustling in the leaves and Fern appeared, looking upset.

'I hoped you'd be here already. There's really bad news. The henhouses have been destroyed - hacked to bits, and all the birds have gone. Every one, including Chanticleer. I'm so sorry, I thought we were keeping him safe for you.' My heart sank. He'd escaped yet again.

'This is terrible. What on earth's going on? I'll come down and have a look.' We made our way to the farm miserably. 'When do you think it happened?'

'I don't know. I only discovered it this morning. But it might have been yesterday as we didn't hear or see anything overnight. It looks like whoever did it had tools; a chainsaw or maybe an axe as the wood is all chopped up. But we'd have heard something like that. So it must have been yesterday. When we were out. I never checked the hens when I got in as it was so late and I assumed Dad had done it.

'Had he been in all day?'

'No, I'd thought he was going to be, but then he went out all afternoon and early evening for something he said.' We arrived at the farm and went round to have a look. Mr. Woodruff was busy clearing up the mess, which was everywhere. He looked grim. There was straw, chicken wire, hen feathers and chopped wood everywhere. The wood didn't look as if it had been sawn, it was, as Fern had said, hacked at, as if by an axe.

'I've just thought ...'

'So've I. That bloke with his axe. He was in a real state when we saw him.'

'Yes. And he avoided me this morning. I bet it's him.'

'I wonder what he's done with the hens. And Chanticleer. Or could they have all escaped of their own accord?'

As if in answer to this question I heard a familiar squawk and looking up at the roof of the farmhouse I saw Chanticleer strutting along the guttering. I almost laughed with relief to know that he was okay. I didn't know he could fly. He couldn't before. His wings had been clipped; they must have grown back. I held up the rowan berries to attract his attention, and he swooped down, proving himself quite capable of flying. But instead of allowing me to catch him again, he snatched the berries in his beak and flew off, this time to the branch of a tree. As I ran over to him, he took off again, now across the fields the other side of the lane, and on towards the river. Fern joined in the chase. He let us catch up for a bit at the river, but remained out of reach on a tree, watching us with his beady eyes, still holding the bunch of berries in his beak. If it hadn't been at such an inconvenient time when we had so much else to do and think about, it would have been almost funny, his behaviour. As it was, it was frustrating and exhausting.

He led us on, up the river where we'd been yesterday, past the cut-down alders and beyond, further than either of us had been. The river was much narrower up here and the banks were very steep. The path had petered out and it was difficult to get along without slipping in.

We scrambled on though, and after a while found ourselves in a small, rocky gorge. Here the water cascaded over big white boulders and the banks became sheer chalky cliffs with only a few ferns and mosses clinging to their sides. 'I've never been in here before,' panted Fern, as Chanticleer hopped about on a pinnacle of rock above her head. He really seemed to be teasing us, or leading us on.

We were having to rock-hop to get anywhere and it was very slow progress. The water was a thin but gushing stream up here. The gorge was very cold, as it was in the shade.

'There's a kind of handrail over there,' I pointed out, crossing over the river to pull myself up on it. 'No it's not, it's a tree root.' It was long and pale, about as thick as my arm. It must have come a long way from the tree it belonged to, as the cliffs were high above us now. It helped us to haul ourselves along the edge of the water and swing across when the rocks were too far apart.

Chanticleer was now perched on a ledge high above our heads. He had put the berries down and was eating a few, as if he had all the time in the world; because it would certainly take us a long time to reach him. We seemed to have come up against a whitish wall of rock in front of us; the water came out of a crack in the rocks that was much too narrow for either of us to carry on through.

'What now?' asked Fern.

'Well he's up there and we're down here. I think he's playing a game with us you know. We have to go on up after him.'

'What, right up there?'

'Well, I'll go and see how easy or difficult it is and call down. This root seems to come from up there somewhere, which is useful.' I pulled myself up the cliff slowly without looking down. It was a bit crumbly, but I made it to the ledge. 'It's okay,' I called down. As Fern pulled herself up with less difficulty than I'd had, I watched Chanticleer out of the corner of my eye. He might not move again until we were both there. This could be my chance if I was careful. With one eye on Fern and one on him, I edged myself along with my hands. I was within a metre of him. I kept very still then rolled swiftly over to grab him. I felt his tail feathers - and missed. He flew right up out of the gorge and over the cliff. I lay back exhausted, and maddened by his behaviour. What on earth was he playing at? Didn't he know what was good for him? Fern scrambled over the edge.

'Gone again, I see. What shall we do, I'm getting pretty hungry now.'

'Me too.' It was well past lunchtime, our trek up the gorge had taken ages. At least it was warm up here as the sun reached in. Then we heard crowing. Turning to look, we could just see the top of a very tall tree above the cliff. It was an ash tree. And perched on the very topmost branch still holding the berries, was Chanticleer. 'Looks like Yggdrasil!' I said.

'Oh you mean Odin's horse!' She knew about everything to do with trees it seemed. 'So that must be one of the roots then ... I wonder where it leads ...' We got up and carried on following the huge root along the ledge, then it disappeared into the cliff. But then Fern noticed something. 'Look - up above where it disappears, there's a hole!' It was quite a big hole, over a metre tall. We moved carefully along the ledge until we were under it. It was just too high to see in. I made a stirrup of my hands and Fern hoisted herself up. 'Wow. It opens right up into a cave.' She wriggled in through the hole and disappeared. Then she re-emerged and stuck out a hand to help me up.

We were in a large limestone cave with stalactites, which narrowed to a tunnel at the far end. Luckily I had my torch and we were able to make our way through it, amazed by all the rock formations. Chanticleer was temporarily forgotten, as there was nothing we could do about him anyway; and this might possibly lead to a way up to the top of the cliff. The ash tree root was still beside us and seemed to have taken over from him in leading us. The tunnel wound gradually upwards I was glad to note, and its surface became drier and more like ordinary rocks. We carried on climbing gradually for a few minutes and came to another cave, with, at last, daylight. One of the walls was a sort of slope of rocks and I could see you could get out if you climbed up it. But Fern had spotted something else. 'Look!' she pointed. The floor sloped away from us and ended in a ledge with less than a foot of space above it. Before I could say anything, she was on her stomach and squeezing herself over the edge of it.

'Hey, wait, we don't need to go that way!' I called. But she had, so I'd have to follow I thought crossly. I shouted, 'What's it like?'

'Don't know can't see anything yet. Give us the torch.' I passed it down and tried to squeeze through to join her. But it was too tight. She was much thinner than me. I couldn't get my shoulders through. I wriggled back up and called down to her. There was no answer. I could hear her footsteps fading into the distance. I silently cursed her, she could have waited. She'd be back, when she realised I wasn't behind her. Then I heard what sounded like a cry, from a long way away.

'Are you okay?' I shouted. 'okay, -kay, -kay' echoed back up to me.' Then silence. I called out a few more times. No answer. I started to worry. She might have hurt herself. I waited. Nothing. This was really bad. Stuck in a cave where no one knew we were, and god knows what had happened to Fern. She could have hit her head and be lying unconscious like I had, but in a cold inaccessible cave this time. I decided to go and get help. Perhaps these caves were well known and there was another entrance somewhere. Surely there must be. I climbed up the rocks to the chink of daylight and pulled myself out into the fresh air.

The bright light was dazzling and I didn't know where I was first of all. Then, looking back roughly the way we had come underground, I saw the top of the tall ash tree where Chanticleer had perched a few hundred metres away. But he was no longer there. I looked out over the landscape. It was thick woodland; there was something a bit familiar about it. Turning round I saw the mound on which Duir stood. I could see him properly now, from a bit of a distance though there were some trees in between. So the ash tree was not that far from Duir and the den. And then I saw that on the very top branches of Duir was that wretched bird, berryless and crowing his head off. No way was I chasing after him now.

I made a note of where I had climbed out of the ground and started walking downhill, in the direction I thought Fern would have gone beneath me. I found myself heading for the base of the hill Duir stood on. Then I noticed other bits of rock and trees were a bit familiar; this was the area I had been lost in during the thunderstorm. In fact, I had just come upon the very tree I came round under after my bash on the head, with all the moss. That made me briefly wonder what I had knocked myself out on before. There were a lot of low branches above my head, and a few boulders, scattered about my feet. Looking closely at these, I suddenly saw a ridge of iron poking out of the soil in front of me. This must have tripped me up - I almost did it again - and caused me to fall and hit my head on the rock down near the tree I'd woken up next to. In front of the ridge of iron was a sudden drop of about six feet.

Carefully, I climbed down a sort of bank beside it and found a lot of old dried branches stacked against it; pushing these aside I discovered to my amazement a very old iron door within an iron frame. It had been the half buried top of this frame I had tripped on. In front of the door a large boulder stuck out of the soil; and between this and the door another smaller rock had been wedged, making the door impossible to open from inside. Breathlessly I tugged the smaller rock out. Now I could open the door. As I did so, I heard voices. Female voices. There was a tunnel in front of me that turned a corner. I hurried quietly along it, and saw flickering torchlight. It was Fern. But not just Fern.

'It's Mum!' she said, her filthy face streaked with tears. 'She's here. She's okay, more or less. My eyes shifted to a skinny woman with long wild hair who Fern was clutching onto.

'Beth?'

'That's me. And you're Louis.' Her face was almost black with dirt and her huge eyes shone in the dim light. 'Thank you for helping to find me.'

'Are you okay?' I asked, not quite sure what to say now this moment had arrived.

'Yes, I'm fine. I could do with a bath though.'

'Mum that's the least of our worries. I'm sorry I lost you

Lou, I suddenly knew Mum was down here and couldn't wait. How did you get in?' I told them. 'That's a relief it's been opened because Mum says he's probably due for a visit soon. We'd better get out and talk later.'

Beth was very weak, but between us we supported her walking to the door. 'Who's due for a visit?' I asked on the way.

'Vince,' said Fern. 'It was him all along. Those cans in the hut, he's been bringing them up to feed her.' I saw empty tins I recognised from the night before lying on the floor. 'And he hasn't been for a few days, she thinks it's likely to be this afternoon as he usually makes it on a Sunday.'

'I kept a tally of the days and weeks,' Beth smiled, producing a little stick with notches scratched on it rather like the one we'd found in the alder tree. Her voice was hoarse with not being used.

'That trail ... did you hope we'd work it out ?' asked Fern as we made our way to the entrance.

'Yes, it was all I could do, knowing you knew a bit about Ogham, not having anything to write with, and not wanting anything that he'd know was me and be able to remove ... I had to do things very quickly, when he wasn't looking.' She was covered in a few old blankets, and when we reached the door she shrugged them off. 'Daylight ... sunlight ... I can't believe I'm seeing it again.' But the light was too bright for her and she had to close her eyes for a few moments. Then she blinked and said, 'I don't think there's any time to lose.' So we shuffled slowly but steadily through the wood to the path that led to the farm.

I wanted to ask so many questions. But we had reached the

edge of the wood and suddenly Fern stopped. 'We're too late. Look.' In the distance a fattish, beer-bellied man was labouring up the field path with a cardboard box in his arms. We quickly retreated into the trees before he could spot us. 'That's him,' said Beth in a trembling voice. 'What shall we do?'

'Hide?' Fern suggested.

I said, 'Or, how about you two hide and I'll go back to the door of the cave and close it up like nothing's happened, and hide close by; then, when he goes inside I'll shut him in with the rocks.'

'Brilliant. But do be careful ... he's not nice. Give him a few moments to get right along the tunnel, but not too long as he'll turn back straight away I'd imagine ... about thirty seconds it used to take from the door - I know, I used to count it,' Beth said.

They headed off round the wood the other way towards school to be well out of the way and I hurried back the way we'd come and replaced the door stone and branches as well as I could in the time.

Then I climbed up the bank and hid in the undergrowth, my heart hammering. I didn't have long to wait. I heard him coming well before he arrived, crashing through the leaves, cursing to himself. The box probably weighed a ton full of tins and presumably water. He dropped the whole thing on the ground and set about removing the branches and stone. I was terrified I would sneeze with all the leaves in my face. Then a banging sound as the door was opened and I started counting. At twenty-five I leapt down, shoved the door shut and quickly got the rock wedged back in place. I tested the door. It was fast. Almost immediately there were footsteps, shouting and hammering. I took off. When I got to the edge of the wood I saw the others had decided to make a dash for it after they'd seen him pass and were nearly at the farm. I hurried down myself.

In the farmyard Beth was in Mr. Woodruff's arms. I was a bit embarrassed but even more so when Fern turned and hugged me. They were all crying. Then Beth broke free. 'Did you manage?' she asked anxiously. I nodded. 'Poetic justice! I'd like to leave him there for weeks now. But I suppose we'd better call the police sooner rather than later.' I said I'd wait for them at the end of the lane. I wanted to leave the Woodruffs on their own.

17 Protest

It should have been a good time, after all that drama and searching; and it was, in that Beth had been found and was alright apart from being a bit weak and shaken; and Fern was obviously much happier. And we were really good friends now we'd been through so much together. I didn't see quite as much of her as the family wanted to spend time together, but that was fine. School was now just tolerable; we both seemed to have got a bit more respect after all that happened.

Yet I had a feeling of it being all over. In a way I missed the excitement of the search we'd been on; it was a bit of an anticlimax. Vince was locked up; I'd told Mum and Dad everything; we'd been in the papers, but were not hassled too much. Fern and I kept quiet about the trees' and Chanticleer's help in our search and of course the den in Duir. She spent a lot of time with her mother and I hung out in the den, doing nothing much, and it was really enjoyable; but here I was more than ever aware that we were losing the wood. If only it *had* been the developers who'd captured Beth we might have stood a chance of stopping them.

But as it was, it was Vince who had been responsible for both kidnapping Beth and all the nasty tricks at the farm. The first thing everyone wanted to know was why. He himself wasn't talking the police said, but Beth had a pretty good idea after being held captive by him all these weeks. After her rescue, Fern and I used to sit with her chatting about it all, as she couldn't do a lot while she recovered from her ordeal. But she said it was good for us to talk about it. 'He thought I was taking Patsy away from him, and making him a laughing stock. She'd been completely under his thumb. But when she began to get involved in the wood protests, she started to realise she could stand up to him about other things too; and she got the job at the museum, and suddenly she was a person in her own right, instead of just someone who cooked Vince's tea and washed his socks. And he didn't like it. He thought she was going to leave him. I think he's got that condition Morbid Jealousy or whatever it's called. So he really hated me from then on, and the family, which was why he did all the nasty things at the farm. He thought we'd move away from the area if we felt threatened enough. But that wasn't enough, so he locked me up too. I learnt all this on his visits; he used to rant and rave at me about it. Sometimes I got scared he'd do something worse to me, but the worst was the day he kidnapped me in the summer after Patsy had visited me with the mended tunic. He tied my legs loosely together and made me walk up to the wood at knifepoint. Then I was terrified. But gradually I realised he was also scared of what he'd done - and scared of me in a way ... he did think I was a witch! And he wasn't planning any more violence on me, just the farm.'

'I feel so sorry for Patsy. She'd been through enough when he was sacked - the shame of it - and he forced her to conceal the existence of the iron age fort I was locked up in, in case people wanted to go up there. Now she knows why.'

'That must have been why she was so jittery when I saw her in the museum,' I recalled.

'You mean jittery because he was making her keep quiet about the fort and pretend it didn't exist, when it was her job to let the public know about things like that. She would have been a lot worse if she'd known why she had to keep quiet,' added Fern. 'But she's moved out of the area now. She can't bear any more gossip.'

'And the irony is Vince *has* lost her now by doing what he did,' said Beth. 'She would have stayed with him even before when he was so foul, but not after what he did to me of course. But I'm sad to have lost her as a friend too. I think somehow she can't face me after what Vince did. And yet that was nothing to do with her.'

'No, but ... if she hadn't obeyed him keeping quiet about the iron age fort, maybe people like me would have gone to look at it, and maybe found you sooner,' I speculated.

'Do you want to know the really annoying thing about the fort? Patsy had been thinking, before I was abducted, that it could be a way of getting a preservation order on the wood. But the developers are going to preserve the fort anyway, as a tourist attraction within the theme part, if you can believe it. So we'll still lose the wood.'

That was the thing that got us all down still, though it

wasn't initially mentioned that much; it felt as if we should just be grateful Beth had been rescued and not hope for more like keeping the wood and all the trees alive, and preserving the den.

'I do feel defeated,' Beth admitted. 'I stood up to the developers, the police, and all that idle gossip, only for one nutcase to break my spirit. If I was physically stronger, it would be different: I think I'd want to have another go. But I'm not yet up to camping out week after week and it's maybe not fair on the family after all they've endured.'

'You're certainly not physically strong enough,' said Mr. Woodruff, who had just walked in. 'Also, there's a chance the business could pick up again now if you put a bit into it, just directing me, which wouldn't tax you too much. Whereas if it's left for another few weeks, we'll probably go under. And the family needs you more right now'.

'Kind of,' said Fern, surprisingly. 'We need to know she's safe and see her frequently; but we don't need to be breathing down each other's necks.' Her parents exchanged puzzled glances. She was frowning as if she had something on her mind.

Later we went up to the den with thick coats, blankets and snacks. It was good being with Fern as she didn't need to chatter away all the time like some girls; like me, she could spend hours lost in a book.

But today she didn't. She continued frowning and thinking to herself, then finally said, 'We can't just give up.'

'What do you suggest?'

'Carry on Mum's battle.'

'Oh yeah, camp out, chain ourselves to trees and all that?'

'If that's what it takes.'

'Are you bonkers?'

She shrugged. 'Nothing ventured, nothing gained. What's the worst that could happen?'

'Oh, just end up in the juvenile courts for truancy, get endlessly grounded by my parents, and with my luck, die of exposure.'

'It's only early October.' There was a tense silence.

'I just think it's mad to think that two children stand a chance against all those powerful adults, especially when a larger number of grown women haven't succeeded, or have only delayed things. And you don't know what my parents are like. They're much heavier than yours.'

'Is that what you're afraid of?' she demanded scornfully, her green eyes blazing.

'No! I just don't know realistically how we'd do it, what we'd be able to achieve. It's just two of us, you know, with no experience of this sort of thing. We'd be on our own.'

A look of exasperation crossed Fern's face. Then she seemed to be listening ... there was an odd but not unfamiliar sensation. A rumbling in the branches we sat in. I knew it was Duir. I pulled off my coat and put it on backwards. Then I heard the words, 'Not alone, not alone ...' as if he hadn't the strength to say more. We looked at each other wonderingly.

'Not alone ...' Fern whispered. Our brief disagreement was instantly dropped; it was like there were more important things to do.

'Okay then', I said finally. 'When do we start?'

'What about Friday? Give us a chance to get used to sleeping out before the workmen start on Monday.'

'Isn't that a bit soon? What do we need to get ready? And are we telling the parents?'

'All Mum's camping stuff is stored in the shed. There are lots of tinned food supplies, sleeping bags, lilos, water bottles and so on. We'll leave the parents a note. It's the only way. If we ask permission we won't get it. They'll go spare of course; it's something we have to expect and deal with. But we haven't got any time to lose - look how much woodland has already been cleared.'

This was true. Sooner than we'd imagined it could become a wasteland. 'How and where shall we challenge the developers?'

Fern outlined her plans. 'I was thinking along the lines of deception; we may only be two kids but if we can pretend there are a number of us, scattered throughout the woods, they won't dare move in case of accidents.'

'You've thought it all through!'

'Kind of. We can make our camp here, where we know there's room and it's comfortable. Then we put things in lots of other trees to make it look like there are people in them ... even maybe rig up a few strings we can pull on to jiggle the branches and so on ... And leave a big notice at the bottom by the portacabins to warn the developers that any further work will endanger lives ...'

'Excellent. And we could do sound effects too, maybe strings that jangle things we hang in the branches, like metal, or wind-chimes ...' I was getting into it now.

'Yeah, and also, we can try and spook them, maybe.'

'We'd better get going then.'

First, we saw to our supplies. We made several trips up to Duir with food, water and bedding. Luckily there was a lot of storage space in the den and on higher branches. It looked so cosy we were looking forward to just spending the night there.

Then we set about making it look like there were lots of us. We tied bits of old clothing to branches and stuck some old curtains I'd found from our farm up likely looking trees as if someone was camping there. And used masses of dark green gardening string, so it didn't show up, to tie to the branches. Then we gathered all the loose ends of string that hung down and tied them to one master string which we unwound as we headed back up to Duir, now our control site. We'd attached some old wind chimes of Beth's, some bits of foil and old CDs, castanets Fern had found in her attic, and pieces of scrap metal that could bang against each other. There were also some gross halloween masks we'd picked up cheaply in town, wedged between branches. In that setting they looked seriously scary - we kept jumping ourselves when we caught sight of them.

It was Thursday after school. All that remained was to let people know about our protest. We sent an email to the local paper telling them how special the woods were, how our town had no other decent green spaces and what an ecological disaster a theme park would be.

Then we turned to the task of the parents. Fern's note was apologetic, but adding 'I know you'll understand' to her mother. That would not do for mine. It would only enrage them further. So I put, 'I don't expect you to understand, but in the end this is so important to me I have to do it.'

On Friday morning on the way to school, I put it in the letter box on the ground floor of Oaklands so they would pick it up that evening. We were going straight from school.

18 Tree Dwellers

The first weekend in the wood was magic. To begin with, that Friday evening, we were nervous of not making it for some reason. We hurried out of school and over the fields as fast as possible. Only when we reached Duir and were inside the den could we start to relax. We set about cooking our tea while it was still light, on the little primus stove. Baked beans and bread had never tasted so good. We followed it with fruit and biscuits and some water. Then it started to get dark so we got the bedding ready on each side of the den. We had two lilos which took a while to blow up, but were really comfy with sleeping bags and blankets on top. We kept most of our clothes on for added warmth - it was great not needing to fuss about baths. We just swished a bit of water round our mouths to do our teeth. Then we snuggled down for a really early night. Both of us had these very long-lasting cool-lite torches so we had the luxury of a read in bed as all the birds settled down around us for the night. But pretty soon we were both tired and switched them off. Fern said, 'I wonder if those strings work.'

Suddenly the wood was filled with a rattling, clanking,

tinkling racket. I nearly jumped out of my skin. 'Don't do that again without warning me!'

'Wimp!' was the cheerful reply. The sound died down gradually in a minute or two. We lay there listening to the relative quiet. Then other sounds stole gradually into our awareness, little rustlings down below, the odd squawk of a bird; in the distance an owl hooted. We felt very safe, though, up in the arms of Duir. It was really warm for October, and a clear night, with stars. Later the moon rose and you could see everything without a torch. We knew a few of the stars like the Great Bear, and the Plough. 'Isn't this alone worth all the agro?' Fern sighed. I agreed. If only we could succeed in our mission as well. All my secret fears about being in the wood at night had lifted. I only had some misgivings about Mum and Dad ... maybe I could get a message to them every so often to say we were okay ... then I fell asleep.

❧

I must have slept really well because the sun was well up the next morning and everything was crisp and fresh. Fern was awake already, busy boiling some water. 'Cup of tea?' she called up. I scrambled down to join her and we had a good breakfast of cereal, tea and bread. 'So far so good then. But the developers won't be at work till Monday; that'll be crunch time. Did you bring the banner?' she asked.

'Mm.' That was our only task for the weekend, besides getting used to woodland life, to put up a big banner I had made on an old sheet, down near the road where passing traffic could see it. It simply said, 'SAVE THE WOOD.'

After breakfast I put our plastic cups and plates and those

from the night before in a bucket and went off in search of the stream I knew started somewhere nearby, to do some washing up. I could hear it in the distance, over towards the ash tree and the iron age fort. Presumably it fed into the river Fern and I had come along when we found Beth.

When I reached it I was surprised to find it was much bigger than I'd expected from when I'd first followed it uphill early in September. The water was crystal clear and collected in a large pool before disappearing into rocks lower down. I washed the dishes and put them to dry in the sun as we hadn't brought a teacloth. Then I felt so warm and the water looked so inviting, I couldn't resist a dip. I decided not test the temperature - I just jumped in in my pants. But it was so freezing I yelled out and Fern came running through the trees to see what was up. She laughed when she saw me, stripped down to her underwear too and jumped in, shrieking. We splashed each other, swam underwater, had short races to warm up, then could stand the cold no longer and rushed out. 'Race you back to camp!' shouted Fern. We grabbed our clothes and went for it. Just as we passed the iron age fort we heard voices. Oh no. It was both sets of parents and Lottie. They were looking very serious, but when they saw us in our dripping underwear they couldn't help laughing. Then they were actually quite nice about it all.

'We are not happy, as you can imagine,' said Mum, trying to sound stern. 'But I brought you these to keep you going for the weekend.' Some Sainsburys sausages, some packet mash, a pack of Mars Delights and a fruit cake in a tin.

'Mum! You're brilliant!' I said and launched myself at her

for a sodden hug. She didn't push me off, though I made her very damp, I think it was so long since she'd had a hug from me. Then Dad said, 'You can stay on condition you come home Sunday afternoon. We've all discussed this and we think you're old enough for a spot of camping. But we want you back well in time to get cleaned up for school.'

'That cake looks yummy, thank you so much,' said Fern quickly. 'May I offer you a cup of coffee to go with a slice?' she giggled, putting on a posh voice.

'We just had one at home thanks,' said her Mum.

'And Beth needs to get back and rest,' said Mr. Woodruff. I looked at Beth. She still looked white and tired, but not unhappy.

'How did you know where to find us?' I asked.

'We thought you might be using the iron age fort,' she said 'but it's been boarded up by the police. Then we heard your voices.'

'Ugh - I wouldn't go in there again!' said Fern.

'Nor me,' agreed her mother, shivering with the memory. We just thought you two mightn't mind and might find it handy. So where are you camping then?'

'In my den,' said Fern quickly. 'It's not far from here, in a very safe, secret place, but it is secret if you don't mind.'

'Okay then,' said Beth. Then the others said goodbye and started going, and she murmured, 'I'm so proud of you both.' Fern's parents were pretty cool about some things compared to mine. They were a good influence on them probably. Dad called back,

'See you Sunday. Did you hear?'

'Yes - I heard,' I replied. We were quiet till they'd gone.

Fern said, 'Heard doesn't mean agreed to.'

'No, exactly. It just means we've heard their point of view. I think they've decided to be kind so that we can do 'a spot of camping,' get it out of our systems, find we miss our home comforts after a bit and come back in time for school. They haven't quite grasped it's not just Swallows and Amazons.'

'Except for Mum perhaps.'

'Yeah.' Now they knew roughly where we were and that we were okay and could cope, I felt okay in turn about Mum and Dad; that even though they wouldn't like it one bit when I didn't come home on Sunday, they didn't have any major cause for worry. So we continued to enjoy our freedom in the woods.

We spent the rest of the morning fixing up the banner down near the road. It was quite tricky and we wanted to make it difficult to remove. But Fern had had the good idea of a stapler and we put loads of staples in all round the edges of the sheet where it was tucked round the steel mesh fence. It was nearly impossible to remove unless you were very patient with a staple-remover. We checked on all our pretend camps and spooked one another until we were laughing so much we could hardly breathe.

'I must ask Mum if she had good times like this while she protested,' Fern said.

We had a snack lunch, and as we felt a bit tired from the morning's efforts, decided to have a quiet read up in Duir. I think we both drifted off a bit. I could feel Duir, as in his vibrations; so could Fern, I could tell, as she glanced at me after each one. We didn't discuss him directly - it seemed kind of rude as he was there and could hear everything; and it didn't seem necessary. I tried reversing my t-shirt which was all I had on, but got nothing more than the vibrations telling us he was still there in spirit as well as physically. I wondered what was weakening him; perhaps it was the threat to the wood. Then thought I heard the words, 'saving myself for later,' but I couldn't quite tell. Saving himself for what?

I must have slept, because suddenly it was cooler and I could hear Fern saying 'let's have a real camp fire tonight. It may be our only chance once the world finds out we're here.'

We cleared away leaves and built a circle of stones with the small rocks that lay around the place. There was plenty of dry kindling from the summer and larger bits of wood to build it up. Pretty soon we had a very satisfying blaze and we decided to do the sausages on it. The mash just needed hot water. It was the best sausage and mash ever and we finished the whole packet between us, then set about the fruit cake. We seemed to have all our meals really early, we were so hungry. So after that, we lay against a little bank enjoying the flames and the warmth of the fire. We felt sleepy and full, with fresh air and food and exercise. The fire crackled and so did the wood; there was a slight breeze that set off a few of the things we'd hung in the trees. 'Didn't think of that, did we, keeping ourselves awake at night,' laughed Fern.

'Don't think anything will keep me awake.' In fact we were really dozy already and the flames dancing in front of my eyes took on strange shapes, like witches and people dancing. I was sure I could hear music - or was it the wind chimes? Then Fern got up slowly and began to dance, her long, loose hair fanning out around her. She circled the fire and I thought I saw her reach out for someone's hand ... it was as if there was a whole crowd of dancers there. I stood up in a trance and my body seemed to move of its own accord, twisting and spinning and writhing with the flames. Fern reappeared around the circle of the fire. She took hold of my hand as she passed, lifted it high and twirled under it, let go and danced on. I followed; my feet seemed to move by themselves. I could see other shadowy figures; the girl I'd danced with in my dream that time on the dancing platform; and other men and women in old costumes. We continued weaving our way around the flames for hours till night fell inky black and the flames died down. Then Fern and I were alone again, silent as we climbed up to bed and fell into the deepest of sleeps.

We slept long and late the next day; eventually I woke to the distant sound of church bells at about eleven. Fern opened her eyes and smiled sleepily at me. I wondered if I'd dreamt the dancing the night before.

We felt like a restful day, so we just hung out round the camp. Cooking and washing up seemed to take a long time and there was nothing more satisfying than reading up in the branches with the sun blazing down. For dinner we had tinned curry and rice - anything tasted delicious out there - and we played a few rounds of cards before reading a bit and settling down for the night.

'They'll be missing us by now,' murmured Fern.

'Yes. I wonder when they'll come looking.' Just then there

was a loud noise. 'Louis! Come out!' It was Dad.

'Ssh, keep still,' whispered Fern. He shouted several more times. 'You'll pay for this!' he ended up bellowing. We held our breath as he passed close to Duir; he must come across the fireplace. But we knew no one could see up into the tree. Torchlight flashed across the branches. Fern put her hand, silencing, onto mine. Then he charged off angrily. I let out a long breath.

It was like the fun bit was over, the battles were just beginning. The weather turned overnight too - the Indian summer was too good to last. In the morning we got up early so we could do things like getting breakfast, before the developers arrived. We were just done, all tidied away without a trace at eight-thirty, when we heard the roar of machinery in the distance. Then there were far-away shouts and it all went quiet. We quickly got up into Duir, carefully replacing the door at the bottom. Next, there were men's voices coming through the trees, rustling the leaves. It didn't sound like Dad. Fern got hold of the string and pulled hard. At once, the woods were filled with an excellent loud racket. There was shouting and the sound of running feet. Fern was delighted. 'Bet we've spooked them!' she hissed. Then we heard them coming closer, several workmen and their boss.

'There's some up in that tree - and some over there too, they're bloody everywhere!'

'We can't do nothing today, it's a friggin' disaster!'

'Bloody greenies!' We smirked silently at each other. It was having the desired effect.

'Oy! Come down from there! You're trespassin'!' one of

them yelled at a bunch of old curtains. We shook with silent laughter. They tramped round for hours, with their threats. Then another one said, 'I don't think there's anyone up there. I ain't actually seen no one.' For an answer, I tugged the string and set off all the contraptions.

'Okay, okay, I know you're there. Just come down so's we can discuss this sensible-like.' Fern shook her head fiercely at me just in case I was silly enough to do as they suggested. We stayed put and jangled the strings every so often to give them a fright. Eventually they went away. It was well past our lunchtime, and we were starving. We took the opportunity to grab a quick bite up in the den. We finished off the last of the bread and cheese; there were only tins left now.

In the afternoon, Dad and Mr. Woodruff came up together. Dad was trying to sound more in control now. He shouted so we could hear wherever we were, but in a steady tone. 'Louis, come out now. This is your last chance to avoid being grounded for the rest of the term.' Mr. Woodruff just called out to Fern to come, like he was begging her. Our eyes met. We found it really hard to keep quiet when they were being reasonable. But having each other strengthened our determination. In the end everyone went away.

It was a cold evening, with a wind that kept all our noise machines in action.

'Couldn't we take them down for the night?' I grumbled.

'But they worked so brilliantly. You'll sleep through them. It's too dangerous to go down and put them up again in the morning,' Fern argued, and she was right again, as usual.

We were going to warm up some more baked beans for

tea. But it turned out the remaining can was not a ring-pull one and we had forgotten to pack a tin-opener. There was hardly anything else to eat, just a bit of fruit cake and one Mars Delight. We shared these and drank lots of water to fill the gap. Then needed to go down for a pee. Luckily the coast was clear. We went to bed in all our clothes and tried to read. But it involved having our hands out of the sleeping bags which let in cold air, so eventually we gave up and tried to sleep. I could hear Fern's tummy rumbling. 'What are we going to do about food then? Can't we get into the tins some other way?'

'Don't know,' she said dully. 'We don't have a very sharp knife or anything do we? Perhaps we could try whacking them on a rock or something in the morning.'

I woke in the night, shivering. It was very noisy with the wind and all our things jangling, and I was really cold. So was Fern - she was also awake. She wriggled closer to try to get warm, but it seemed like it was dawn before we got back to sleep. The cold soon woke us again. We had a cup of tea but there wasn't anything else for breakfast, so we felt tired and hungry before the day had begun.

Quite early, we got a visit from the police, with dogs. This felt pretty threatening, like they really meant business. We could also hear the developers, Dad's and Mr Woodruff's voices. The dogs led them to the foot of Duir, whining and barking, and snuffling at the trap door. We had made this extra secure the night before, wedging a rock behind it, so it couldn't be pushed inwards, but they knew we were up there from the dogs' behaviour. 'Okay kids, game's up,' said one of the older policemen. 'Time to come down before we come and get you.' He shone a torch up through the branches. There were fewer leaves now and some of the brushwood had been blown down in the night. I found myself dazzled by a light directly in my eyes as I peered down. 'The lad's there!' he shouted triumphantly. 'Down you come then and tell us what you've done with the little girl.' He seemed to have got hold of the wrong end of the stick, and this enraged Fern. She shouted,

'I'm not a little girl; he hasn't done anything with me. We're padlocked to the branches and the key is impossible to find. We're not coming down till we get a written promise to leave our wood alone!' There was an exasperated muttering down below, then,

'We'll be back!' And they went. They didn't come back for the rest of the day, nor was there any sound of machinery being used. Fern was triumphant.

'See. We're winning. We've just got to hold out now. They don't know what to do. They think we're locked here with padlocks and they're terrified of being sued if they hurt us. Should've brought some chains and things to make it look more convincing. We've just got to hang in here.'

But it was not much fun hanging in or out in the now quite wintry weather, having not eaten and with no prospect of doing so. I'd had no luck with the tins. Tonight was not only cold, but it rained as well. We were partially sheltered but even so it was damp and miserable.

We were woken from a dreadful night's sleep, frozen and faint with hunger, by two policemen and the developer.

'We've decided to halt all construction on this site for the foreseeable future, on condition that you come down and return to your homes.' Fern and I gazed at each other in bleary amazement, wondering if it was a trick.

'I said we wanted it in writing!' she shouted finally.

'We have a letter to this effect, Miss,' said the other policeman.

'Show us then.' They held up a sealed letter. No way were we going down to get it. Then I had the idea of lowering a length of string down. The guy got the idea and tied the letter to it. We pulled it up. It said exactly what they had said. It had a police letterhead and was signed by both the police and the developer.

'Looks pretty genuine to me,' I said. Fern nodded. 'Do you trust them?'

'No further than I could spit.' she said scornfully. 'But if it's in writing they'll have to abide by it, else they could be taken to court and so on ...' This seemed reasonable to me. 'But we don't want them to know where the entrance to the den is,' she added.

I shouted down, 'Go back to the road and we'll meet you there.' They muttered to themselves, then agreed and tramped off the way they'd come.

It seemed too good to be true. We quickly packed up our clothes and books, deciding to leave the bedding and camping stuff for possible future use. We wrapped it all in bin liners to keep it dry and pushed it into the large storage spaces.

There was a police car waiting by the road. We were surprised to see most of the workmen hanging around as well as the developer. 'Okay, where's the rest of them?' asked the policeman who was driving the car.

'There's just us, said Fern. They exchanged glances.

'Clever little buggers aren't you? In we get then, you'll be home in no time for a hot bath and a spot of breakfast.'

'Patronising idiot,' murmured Fern. They were treating us like six year olds. We got in, either side of a policeman in the back, did up the seatbelts and the car roared forward.

At almost the same moment, there was a roar of machinery starting up. We looked out in horror. It all swung into action and the clearing started again. Fern went berserk. 'You lying bastards! Stop the car!' She threw herself forward - I didn't know what she meant to do to the driver, but the man between us pulled her back.

'Steady on. You're in enough hot water already without causing an accident.' She writhed violently to get his arm off her.

'Just wait till this is in the papers! We'll see you lot in court!'

The policemen laughed. 'That's as maybe, but not before these people have finished their work which is within the law and for the public's benefit. You two, on the other hand, you're in big trouble for truancy and wasting police time.'

I had never felt so angry or so powerless in all my life. I felt like punching their lights out. Fern and I could not see each other easily because of the fat policeman between us, and they dropped her off at the farm first to her waiting parents so we did not get a chance to talk. Then they took me back to the flats.

It was only Dad at home. 'Where's Mum?' I said bleakly.

'Working. What do you think? You want us to lose our jobs as well as get fined for your truancy, as well being worried sick about what's happening to you? Get to your room; get ready for school in five minutes. I can't trust you an inch Louis. You're staying in for the rest of the term. There's no pocket money - it's going towards the fine.'

I went to school where I was given detention for the rest of the month - which fitted in with Dad's plans not to let me enjoy myself ever again - and fell asleep in the afternoon. Fern had at least been allowed to catch up on her sleep at home, so I couldn't see her, and they still weren't on the phone again yet.

19 A Prophecy Fulfilled

I had thought the worst week of my life was when we sold the farm; but then, I'd still had hopes we might move somewhere reasonable. Then, when we arrived at this place, the yuck estate complete with Farrow and Co., and the really crap school, all the rowing and Dad being so moody, well, then I thought things couldn't get much worse. But I was wrong - then I'd had the escape of the wood and the comfort of the trees, and after a while, Fern. Now, it was worse. I couldn't go to the wood and soon that was to be taken from us; I was grounded and couldn't go to the farm and see Fern; I was in permanent detention and had no pocket money even if I'd been able to go anywhere to spend it; and the biggest thing of all was that there was no prospect of anything getting any better. We had failed in our protest and still felt angry and humiliated by the dirty trick played on us; loads of people at school seemed to think it was a great joke. When I did talk to Fern briefly at break or lunch, she was in an equally bad mood, so we weren't much comfort to each other. I felt especially cut off from Dad, who seemed to have forgotten that I'd been nice to him when he was down. Now he was just cross and telling me what to do without listening to my point of view. Mum was a bit better. She could understand what we were trying to achieve, but said I should not have made out to Dad we would come back on Sunday and then stayed. She said that was going back on our word just like the police had. I could sort of see that, though did not admit it to her.

Fern's parents had a different attitude, I learnt, during our post-mortem at break the day after we came back. Fern herself was very bitter and angry but swore she wouldn't let it drop. 'But now I've got no spare time at all to do anything, nor can you, being grounded. Mum and Dad said they sympathised with our protest, but not our disobedience. Mum even said she was proud of us again, but I would have to take the consequences of my actions, along with getting tired and hungry in the wood: and that these included paying the truancy fine. I have this paper round after school everyday, and I've calculated that it will take all year. But we're not giving up.'

I didn't see what else we could do since we both had no time or freedom to protest. I was cooped up in the flat all the time I wasn't at school. The evenings weren't light for long after school now, so probably I would have stopped going to the woods anyway during the winter weeknights. But there were still weekends, which I now spent indoors doing extra homework. I wasn't even allowed television, not that I'd watched that much before. It was a dismal time, the worst yet.

So I went on the internet, under the pretence of homework. I read masses more about trees and found we weren't the only ones passionate about them. There were all the websites devoted to Celtic mythology, some of which were fascinating, some just weird; I remembered all the things round Beth's study. And there were protest sites, too. I wished we'd known a bit more about the whole business before we'd been been tricked and we might have avoided it. We weren't the only ones, it seemed. There was a situation a bit like ours but on a larger scale, in New Zealand. Apparently a city council decided to chop down a splendid avenue of trees; when protesters chained themselves on platforms to the trees they were persuaded down by the promise to leave the trees alone; and like our situation, as soon as they'd descended, the men rushed in with chainsaws. There must be some other way, I thought to myself ... maybe start my own website ... but that would be too late for our wood. I would talk to Fern again.

When we met at break, she said that the felling hadn't got very far because the weather had been bad. She gave me a note. 'This is from my parents, inviting yours to dinner tomorrow. 'Cos we still can't afford the telephone!'

I took it. 'Huh, alright for some. And I'm supposed to babysit Lottie while they go off and enjoy themselves, I suppose.'

'Well charge them: tell them what the going rate is. Say you can't afford to do things for free anymore as you have a fine to pay off !'

The next day after detention I got home just as Mum and Dad were getting ready to go to Wheelers Farm. It was a really windy night, it reminded me of the time I'd got caught in the storm in the woods. Dad was anxious. 'Maybe we should put off going tonight.'

'Oh no, we'll be fine in the work truck. I've been so looking forward to it. Our first meal out in how long? And we can't cancel as they're not on the phone.' said Mum.

'Do go,' said Lottie seriously, and that seemed to decide it. As soon as they were out of the door she led me to her room where she had a Barbie game waiting in her wardrobe. Two of the dolls were poking out of her dressing gown pockets. 'This is the wood,' she explained, gesturing to the hanging clothes, 'and this is you and Fern in the tree. I'm going to talk Fern and you can talk you.' I sighed, not feeling like playing with dolls right then. But as usual, she persuaded me and somehow I got right into it. Lottie was shouting 'You're not going to cut my trees down!' and she made her Barbie throw coathangers down on imaginary police. 'Now you can go to prison yourself Mr. Policeman.' I wondered what she'd been told about our protest while we were away. I put her to bed after an hour or so and she went straight to sleep, contented with her game; I lay awake for a bit, listening to the wind and half expecting my parents at any moment, who had said they wouldn't be late. Eventually, I fell asleep.

Later I was woken by a lot of noise. There were dustbins rolling and clanging on the concrete outside; the wind was really howling and it felt as if the whole block of Oaklands was going to take off. When I looked out of the window I was gobsmacked. All kinds of stuff was flying through the air: cardboard, branches, bits of fence; and then I looked down to the garages and saw their roof had been ripped off by the force of the gale. A small tree lay uprooted by the side of the road. Suddenly there was a white explosion of lightning and almost in the same instant the most enormous thunderclap sent me reeling back from the window. The lightning seemed to scorch my eyeballs and I could see nothing else for a few minutes as I fled back to bed. It was the most violent storm I'd ever experienced. I pulled the blankets round my ears like I used to when Mum and Dad had their rows ... Mum and Dad. Had they got back alright? If they had, they wouldn't appreciate me barging in on them; and if they hadn't, there was not much I could do about it. The thunder and lightning went on and on. I couldn't shut it out with the duvet and fingers in my ears. It seemed to be directly overhead still and I wished we were not on the top floor.

Eventually there was a bit more of a gap between the lightning and the thunder and I poked my head out of the covers. It was pitch black, without the usual streetlight shining in. There must have been a powercut. It would probably be in the flats as well. But then I noticed a strange burning smell. I didn't like this. I needed to know if Mum and Dad were safe or not.

I got up and felt my way to the door. The moment I opened it I smelt smoke. There was a fire in the sitting room and the corridor was filled with smoke, choking, chemical smelling stuff. I slammed the door shut again, shaking. I looked round for something to put over my mouth. My swimming stuff. It hadn't been unpacked from two days ago and was still a damp soggy bundle. The smell of chlorine was clean compared to the corridor. I wrapped the towel round my head and mouth, threw on my new jacket for extra protection, and made a dash for Mum and Dad's room. Their bed was empty. I really panicked then. The front door was through the sitting room. No way could I get through. I had to get Lottie. But the phone was in Mum and Dad's room so I picked it up first in case I didn't get another chance and dialled 999, feeling for the 0 at the bottom as I couldn't see a thing in there. When I got through a woman told me to stay calm and keep the doors and windows shut because there was a delay getting fire engines through. She said loads of trees had come down and were blocking the roads, but they would be with me eventually. Great.

Now I had to reach Lottie. Shaking with fear I made a dash for her room which was right at the other end of the smoke-filled corridor. I couldn't remember if I'd shut her door and kept my fingers crossed. I had. I rushed into her room and slammed the door behind me. To my horror she just lay there in the bed. Had the smoke got the better of her? We'd just had this fire lecture at school and they said that was what got most people. Then I realised she was only asleep. Please be okay, I prayed as I tried to wake her. She always slept so deeply. Eventually she woke. She was surprisingly calm when I told her the flat was on fire. 'We can get out the window,' she said.

'They're not the sort that open ... and it's a long way down.' I tried her window but it didn't move.

'The bathroom one does.' She was right. I hadn't thought of that. But the noise of the fire was much louder now and we could feel the heat of it even through the walls. I was afraid to go out in the corridor again. But it was our only chance. I picked Lottie up and wrapped the towel round both our faces. Then I told her to take a deep breath and hold it as long as she could. I opened the door and we made a dash for the bathroom which was at the other end of the corridor on the far side of the flat away from the fire. It was a bit clearer in there; even so we were coughing and gasping after I'd shut the door. At least there was water here. I wetted the towel and wiped our faces. Then I climbed on the bath and opened the window to fresh night air filled with rain. The fire didn't seem to have reached this side of the building yet. I looked down and saw the pipes from all the flats' bathrooms down this side. But the wind was still ferocious. I got onto the sill with difficulty and was nearly blown off. No way could I get myself and Lottie down in this gale without falling. And it was so high, you'd break more than a leg.

Trembling, I climbed down and sat on the side of the bath, holding Lottie in my arms. 'The firemen will come and rescue us soon, I'm sure,' I said, though I didn't see how they could possibly get here in time if the road was blocked. The noise of the fire had become terrifying now. We could hear things exploding in the flat - the telly and computer probably. Smoke was starting to come under the bathroom door which was not close fitting, and through the ventilation brick. That must mean it was inside the walls on this side too. It was only a matter of time.

'I'm scared,' Lottie whimpered. I didn't tell her I was terrified, just hugged her tighter. We were both crying. I thought of Mum and Dad. How they would feel if they were alive and we weren't. I couldn't imagine how it would feel. I knew, suddenly, in that moment, that they would be devastated and that all their strictness was because they did love me. And that I shouldn't have gone back on my word to Dad. I was openly bawling now into Lottie's fragrant no-tears shampooed hair. Part of me wanted to protect her from knowing what was about to happen as long as possible; but in the end, when the end came, I didn't want her to feel I'd deceived her. I sat her on my lap, and kissed her on both cheeks.

'I love you Lottie, lots and lots.'

'Me too,' she sniveled. Then I got us to the window, because it was getting hard to breathe in there. I held her up and we gasped in the fresh air. Then Lottie said, 'Look. The trees are moving.' She was pointing towards the wood. Our eyes had become adjusted to the dark a bit, and the black outline of the top of the wood could just be picked out against the blue-black sky. The thunderstorm had passed, but not the tremendous wind. Then I saw what she meant: the line where the tops of the trees met the sky was moving towards us. The whole hillside was moving with a loud roaring sound, towards the flats. 'I don't like it!' screamed Lottie. We watched, mesmerised. Trees seemed to be falling everywhere, crashing and splintering, their rootballs hurtling through the air and all the time getting closer and closer. Then there was a slight lull, as if they'd got as far as possible; but almost immediately this was followed by a huge crash as the whole window was filled with a gigantic tree that was closer than all the rest and falling with a deafening creaking and groaning towards us. We jumped back from the window just as it hit the building with an ear-splitting bang. Lottie screamed and I could feel vomit rising in my mouth. Then all we could hear was an almost musical tinkling as window after window splintered and shattered far below. Cowering in the corner near the smoky door we could see a branch sticking through into the bathroom. It had a few papery leaves still attached. It was an oak tree. Cautiously I went over to the window, got back on the bath and peered out. I could see the branch led to the trunk, an enormous one, that had come to rest at an angle against the building. It swayed a bit, then seemed to settle. There were many other branches near to the one in the window. I gave this one a hard push. It didn't budge.

'Lottie, I think we can get out on this tree.'

The first bit, getting out of the window itself, was the hardest, as the opening was now so small. But once I was onto the tree and had hauled Lottie through, we were able to walk down the branch holding onto the one above it. I went first, with one arm under her arms in case she slipped. We both had bare feet but the bark was slippery with the rain, and the drop was terrifying. 'Just don't look down,' I told her. But it was hard not to as you had to look where to put your feet.

And then a window beside me exploded and huge flames leapt out. A piece of glass flew into my face and I could feel hot blood gushing down it. But no pain. 'It's okay Lottie, keep going,' I gasped. We were about half-way down. Then we heard sirens. 'It's the fire-brigade!' The flames were now in the top branches of the oak tree, which were blazing away, and had reached this side of the flats. Soon the branches would snap off as they burnt and the tree might shift. We had to be quick. In the distance I could see the fire engines now hurtling towards us. We scrambled on down as fast as we could, along thicker and thicker branches. Then I saw the whole tree was split by a great charred gash in the trunk: it had been hit by the lightning. It started to rock suddenly as a branch came crashing down to the ground. Lottie started to say, 'There's all your camping stuff Lou-' when she slipped. I leant out and grabbed her arm with one hand, and grabbed a higher branch to balance myself. It turned out to be scorching hot and was agony to hold but I couldn't let go or we would both have fallen. It was only a few seconds probably, but felt like hours of white hot pain. And then it was all over. A man's voice said, 'you're okay now lad,' and Lottie and I were both lifted down a ladder to safety. As I came down I saw the remains of Fern's den. It was Duir who had saved us. But this was the end of him. Stupidly, the moment my feet touched the ground I ran back and threw myself over his great warm trunk sobbing. They thought I was disturbed because of our ordeal no doubt, and picked me up and took Lottie and me to the ambulance waiting to take us to hospital.

20 Chanticleer's Wood

When I woke the next day I was in a white hospital bed with lots of tubes everywhere. Lottie was sitting at the end of it, looking solemn. 'You nearly died, Lou.'

'It wasn't that bad. Might have done if you hadn't had the clever idea of getting to the bathroom window. Reckon that saved us both.' That and Duir, I thought sadly. She looked pleased with herself. A nurse came round the curtain.

'The hero's awake then!'

'Don't know about that' I muttered. 'Where's my parents?'

She looked guarded. 'They've not yet arrived, but I'm sure it won't be long now. There's been the biggest storm you can imagine and many of the roads are still blocked and the phones are down. It's chaos out there, but I'm sure your Mum and Dad will get here as quickly as possible.' I did not quite trust her.

'Is Lottie okay?'

'She's absolutely brilliant. Look at her. All down to your bravery we heard from the firemen!'

'Why've I got all these tubes and bandages?'

'Painkillers, mainly, and fluids you need. You've got a few

cuts and burns, one nasty one on your hand. We'll need to keep you in for a little bit, but you'll soon be right as rain. I'll just top up your drip then get you a bit of breakfast.' The storm and the fire started to come back to me. I became aware that my hand did hurt a lot. The nurse came back with toast.

'There's no weetabix,' said Lottie sadly. Then a social worker came to see me. She was even more jolly and and asked a lot of questions about us and about Mum and Dad. At one point she said, 'I'm afraid you don't have a home to go back to, but not to worry, you won't be out on the streets, we've got some very reasonable temporary accommodation you can go to. And you'll be here for a bit anyway till you're better. Now, getting back to your parents, why did they leave you on your own with your sister last night?'

I had suddenly had enough of this busybody person. 'Because I'm well capable of looking after her while they go out to dinner, as I think I've shown last night. Now if you don't mind I'm tired and need to rest.' She looked a bit taken aback by this, but couldn't really argue, and scuttled off to do more good deeds elsewhere. I didn't like her. I could see she thought Mum and Dad were neglectful parents and was trying to worm it out of me. I just wanted them back. So did Lottie.

'I wish Mummy was here!' She came and clambered into my high, white bed in all the funny clothes the hospital had given her. We snuggled up together and she sucked her thumb and began to doze.

And then the door burst open and in came Mum and Dad. I had never been so glad to see them. And never seen them look so funny. They were covered in mud, Dad's trousers were in shreds and Mum's hair looked like a bird's nest. She flung herself on us, waking a delighted Lottie, and Dad came round the other side and did the same. We all laughed and cried. It was really wet. But I was so relieved they were alive. 'How d'you get like that?' I asked when I could speak.

'We walked here across country. Got to the flats after a few hours, and found they were burnt down. We were beside ourselves with worry for a short time till we met that guy from downstairs with the skip who said he'd seen the fire-brigade rescue you last night and the ambulance take you away. Of course we were desperate to know if you were okay, which we only just found out on our arrival here, which took another three hours. It's chaos out there; the roads are still blocked.' Dad looked grey with exhaustion. 'We spent the night at the farm; you couldn't get out of the house the wind was so violent. We knew you would be sensible and look after Lottie; we had no idea about the fire till this morning, which was just as well ...'

We talked for hours, until the nurse came and said I needed to rest and have some tea. Then she said they could stay with us, but she'd run out of camp beds. There had been so many admissions and so many people with nowhere to go. Lottie still had a bed next to mine, so eventually Mum and her shared that and Dad said he was fine with a pillow and blankets on the floor next to me. They went off to have a shower. Somehow the day passed in a flash, and I was ready to sleep again early - the painkillers were making me drowsy. I waited till Dad got back and settled down. We chatted away quietly.

Dad said, 'I thought so much about you, during the storm, when we were trapped at the farm. I was thinking I'd been too hard on you. I did actually admire you and Fern for standing up for something you believed in; as your Dad I couldn't allow you to stay off school, and I felt let down by you going back on your word; but I also understand why you did it.'

'I was thinking too, while we were stuck in that bathroom … I'm sorry for that bit.'

'It's okay. All that matters to me now is that you're safe. Those woods are magnificent aren't they? A lot of the trees came down in the landslide, but most of them are still there, I noticed this morning.'

Having Dad there again made it easier to cope with the idea that Duir would not be around. It felt right that Duir should remain between Fern and I; but I told him about the special tree that had been our den and had enabled to us to escape the fire. Dad thought it an amazing coincidence it had moved so far in the landslide - and ended up right by our flat. Then I remembered something. 'My new jacket!'

'I wouldn't worry about a jacket,' said Dad, surprised.

'No, it had some of that oak tree's acorns in the pocket; I particularly wanted to plant them.'

'There's a bin bag of all your's and Lottie's clothing over here.' He reached out and untied it.'Phew! What a stink of smoke. Here it is. Yes, stuffed with acorns still.' Then I felt suddenly okay about everything and went to sleep at last.

We spent a strange but quite happy few days in the hospital while the world outside recovered too. We watched it all on telly in the patients' lounge. It was truly mind-boggling.

Our wood wasn't the only one to suffer; loads of ancient trees around the country had also been destroyed. People said it was like the Day of Judgment - but judgment for what? I felt like I knew: for trying to destroy the green world. Then I remembered the words I'd heard:

When Duir comes to the king
Then shall cease all manner of thing
The evil dwelling shall be consumed
the poisoned land entombed
by thunder bolt and lightning flame
Viriditas once more shall reign.

It seemed like a prophecy that had come true. The evil dwelling and the poisoned land - surely the estate, the blocks of flats with their asbestos ceilings, now destroyed and entombed, buried in the landslide. Thunder and lightning had played a part in wiping them out; but, 'Duir comes to the king'? Of course, Kingsmead. At the museum in town I had read that the estate was built on fields known as the King's Meadow, where royal jousting tournaments used to be held. Duir had literally come to Kingsmead, fulfilling his promise to protect me, and had died in the process. But then I remembered how old he was and how weak; it was more like he had been hanging on until this happened, like he knew it would happen. I recalled him saying that the trees could sense 'the shape of things to come.' He had also implied I had a part to play in this great, cleansing, regenerating upheaval. Well I had tried, unsuccessfully, to save the wood. But I did have his descendants in my pocket. Now I had to fulfil my part of his prediction, help ensure viriditas could reign again. Maybe I would have to start a new wood somewhere. It would not be the same. But better than nothing.

After a few days we had some visitors: The Woodruff family. Everyone squashed around my bed and talked and talked about what happened and what would happen. Then Beth said, 'We wondered if you'd come back and live in one of the labourers' cottages. You're welcome to those whatever, while you sort things out; but there's something else: we need a bit of help with the business. We thought we could diversify a bit and try some animals, and thought with your family's experience ... we've a lot of spare land.'

'Yes!' shouted Lottie and Fern and I together. Mum and Dad looked at each other and nodded slowly. 'Yes please,' said Mum, and we all laughed at how quickly it was decided. Fern and I beamed at each other ecstatically. It made financial sense all round from the adults' point of view; it would give Fern's parents much needed support, and Mum and Dad could keep their jobs for a while and start off with a few animals. I said I would do a lot of the looking after of the animals, as I knew how to very well, and so did Lottie.

They all left that afternoon to go to the farm. There seemed little point them hanging around taking up room in the hospital. I felt a bit out of it - I would have liked to be there when they moved in. But the doctor had said my hand needed at least another week before I could be discharged. Mum came back the next morning and said I was better off here for the time being; there wasn't enough bedding and there was a lot they needed to make it comfortable, but they were going to get stuck into all that during the next few days.

When she had gone, I rolled Duir's acorns around in my burnt hand. I closed my eyes and tried to imagine his voice. I was wearing this funny hospital gown which already looked back to front. With some difficulty I wriggled it round the other way. Then I lay back again and relaxed, feeling the acorns, smooth and cool against my blistered skin. After a while they became warm and my hand seemed to throb, but not painfully. And then I heard the words, 'viriditas ... viriditas.' Duir was still with me.

It was twilight when the nurse's voice woke me from a long sleep. 'Well what is it with the gown then? Let's have a look at that dressing.' I hated this bit, seeing my oozy, blistered hand, and it hurt. They had stopped giving me painkillers now. But when she undid the dressing it came off easily. 'My god - it's a miracle!' she gasped. 'How you kids can heal.' My hand was almost completely better. 'Well I expect Doctor will let you go home.' And he did. They needed the beds.

The family were as delighted as I was. Mum and Dad had Special Leave from their jobs. Dad collected me in the work van and drove us to Wheeler's Farm. It looked as beautiful as the day I'd first seen it, with smoke rising from the chimneys straight up into the autumn air. But better cared for. The paintwork was cleaned up, the wisteria pruned and the trellises repaired. The yard was swept and the hen houses had been fixed up (the hens had all come back, as had Chanticleer who ruled the roost once more) and even the kitchen garden was taking shape.

I wasn't prepared for how nice the cottages had been made inside. In the end we had two out of the three of them, as they were very small. As you walked in there was a kitchen with red stone floor tiles just like our old kitchen, and a pine table with a big feast spread out on it. In the middle was a cake which Lottie had helped Mum to ice, saying, 'Welcome Home Louis' There was a cosy sitting room next door and Mum and Dad had been to Ikea and filled it with bright cushions and rugs and shelves. But the best bit was my new bedroom upstairs. It was a decent size, with a large window looking out to the woods. There was a new bed, desk and bookcases, and Mum had found some fab animal posters she'd put round the walls. 'If you don't like them you can change them,' she said anxiously. But I didn't want to. There was a big yellow rug over the old, stripped floorboards, which matched the bright yellow walls. 'It's so cool! even better than my old room before we moved,' I exclaimed, and flung myself on the bed to test it. It was really comfy, until Lottie threw herself on top of me.

Then the Woodruffs came over for my welcome home tea, and Fern came bounding in, her eyes shining. Dad said, 'We weren't allowed to tell you the best news until Fern came.'

Fern said, 'Right. Number one. My parents are so filthy rich now yours are paying a little rent and turning the business around, that they can afford to send me back to my old school. And - this is the cool bit - the headmaster said he'd read about you in the papers, twice now, and said he always had room, and probably a bursary, for exceptional people like yourself. So your parents say you can come too if you want!' Did I ever.

'Can I?' I asked Mum and Dad anxiously. They laughed

and said it was all arranged. This was major. Fern had often told me how nice the place was.

'But number two: this is the best news ever!' she almost shouted. 'The developers can't go ahead with the theme park now! Because of the landslip, it's thought to be unsafe, and the Council has just decided it needs to preserve the wood and the iron age fort itself!'

I was speechless for a moment. 'What made them decide that?' I asked, looking at Dad.

'I had a few words in the right places,' he admitted. 'But after everything that's happened it was obvious it was the right thing to do.. They also asked me to come up with a name for it and I thought it should be 'Chanticleer's Wood.'

Fern and I did a triumphant war dance round the table and Lottie joined in shouting, 'Shonty's Wood has won! '

We had a brilliant meal, all seven of us. It was the first of many we were to share. Afterwards Lottie was put to bed and the parents sat in the sitting room with a bottle of wine, talking farm stuff. Fern and I went up to my new room and played some music.

'You know, it was all worth it wasn't it?'

'You bet. By the way will you come with me to the wood tomorrow?' I showed her the acorns.

'Of course. But you'll get a bit of a shock.'

☙

We went up the familiar field path from the farm the next morning. There were lots of flattened fences and fallen trees everywhere. It took us a while to reach the woods. On this side they weren't too bad. We circled round to the iron age fort, which was still boarded up, and undamaged. Then we reached the place where Duir had stood. 'Be careful,' warned Fern. Suddenly there was nothing; just a gaping crater where Duir had been, and from there on the whole hillside was missing it seemed. It looked horrible after the peaceful place I'd known; like an opened grave or something. In the distance the estate looked like an atomic bomb had fallen on it. Not that I minded that. But in the wood back near to where Duir had been, the soil was still there, though all churned up.

'I think this is the place to plant Duir's descendants.' I said. We each took a handful of acorns and walked along the top edge of the landslip, throwing them in at wide intervals. It seemed like scattering someone's ashes. Afterwards, we were quiet and sat down near the edge. 'It's not going to be the same, is it?' I said.

'No, not the same. But - I want to show you something.' I followed Fern, wondering what now.

She led me up past the fort, over the ridge which had the caves beneath it, and up to the huge ash tree we'd christened 'Yggdrasil.' Not far away, we could hear the gorge roaring down to the valley, now swollen with all the rain after the storm. 'What do you think?' she asked.

'Think about what?' But then I looked at the tree, and saw what she meant. It had far reaching views and a wide space at the base of its crown where thick branches stuck out. It was ideal for a new den. 'I think it's a great idea. Let's get to work this afternoon.'

The End

A Few More Words About Trees

The legends ascribed to particular trees in this book are all 'real' in the sense that they were widely held beliefs a long time ago. The Ogham tree alphabet was also widespread and there are many surviving examples on sticks and standing stones.

Can trees make sounds? The 'listening tree' at Kew Gardens allowed people to listen to the sounds inside it as it drew up water and nutrients through the trunk, by listening to headphones amplifying the sounds from those parts inside the tree. How about lighting up the way for someone who is lost? If you try staring at tree branches then close your eyes you can get an afterimage of the branches behind closed eyes. Then it may be a matter of relaxing deeply in order to sense the right direction to take. What about healing? There is quite a bit of evidence that physical and mental healing can speed up when a person relaxes in a natural environment. This is just one of the many reasons why we cannot afford to lose our woodlands.

The Ogham Tree Alphabet

Letter	Symbol	Name	Tree
B	T	Beth	Birch
L	TT	Luis	Rowan
F	TTT	Fern	Alder
S	TTTT	Sail	Willow
N	TTTTT	Nion	Ash
H	⊥	Huath	Hawthorn
D	⊥⊥	Duir	Oak
T	⊥⊥⊥	Tinne	Holly
C	⊥⊥⊥⊥	Coll	Hazel
Q	⊥⊥⊥⊥⊥	Queirt	Apple
M	╱	Muin	Vine
G	╱╱	Gort	Ivy
nG	╱╱╱	nGetal	Broom
St	╱╱╱	Straiph	Blackthorn
R	╱╱╱╱	Ruis	Elder
A	✝	Ailm	Fir
O	╫	Onn	Furze
U	╫╫	Ur	Heather
E	╫╫╫	Eadhadh	Aspen
I	╫╫╫╫	Idhadh	Yew

ACKNOWLEDGMENTS
Special thanks to Ann, Anna, Nicola and Geoff
for all their patient help, encouragement and expertise.

Lightning Source UK Ltd.
Milton Keynes UK
UKOW030231150513

210691UK00004B/10/P

9 780957 481800